Long Ball to Left Field

DUANE DECKER

Long Ball to Left Field

WILLIAM MORROW AND COMPANY

NEW YORK 1958

For Mike McNamara—

friend, landlord, and non-severest critic,

whose hospitality helped get this book written.

Long Ball to Left Field

1

MIKE JAFFE said he'd always thought Babe Ruth might have gone a lot farther in baseball if he'd stuck to pitching. He said this to Jug Slavin, manager of the world champion Blue Sox, who had beaten the Robins the previous October in five games, to win the title plus the winner's share of the gate receipts. Jug barely smiled.

The remark was made behind the batting cage at the Sox spring-training camp in Glensota, Florida, when Jug told Mike that the front office wanted him to try to convert from pitcher to outfielder this year. Mike shook his head no.

Mike never made funny remarks; he spoke every word in dead earnest. Jug Slavin was aware of this and was tempted to point out the humor in the comment. On the other hand, Mike Jaffe represented valuable property to the Sox; they had paid him a sixty-thousand-dollar bonus to sign with them, out-bidding seven other teams. Mike was twenty now, a pro for three years. He still had the sixty thousand, or what the government had left him of it, in the bank, and he felt reasonably independent. Jug, whose contract expired this year, didn't.

"Look," Jug said. "Think about it."

"No," Mike said. "The Sox can't convert me, not after I wasted half my life learning to pitch."

Jug still didn't crack a smile, not even at the thought that a twenty-year-old boy might really feel he had wasted half his life. "I'll put it this way," Jug told him. "The front office is offering you a chance to break into the starting line-up of the team the sports writers all pick to repeat. I mean, World Series dough. You don't want it?"

"I'm a pitcher," Mike said.

Jug Slavin looked out across the ball park, at the waving Florida palm fronds beyond the left-field fence. He knew very well that he had exaggerated the case for the Blue Sox when he'd said the sports writers had picked them to repeat. They had, but with the usual sports writer's big "if."

"If," they had said, practically in concert, "they

can find an outfielder who can hit that long ball to left field the way Kennie Willard has been doing it for nearly ten years."

Kennie Willard had simply quit—and with good reason. Ever since he had broken into the Sox line-up, the first Negro to knock down the old racial barriers, he had been clean-up man. He was thirty-eight now, and this past winter he had gone into business, making more than the Sox could offer him. He had known he was slightly over the hill, although he could have carried on for a few more years, shifting to third, pinch-hitting, and all that. But he was too good a ballplayer, too proud, to round out his career that way. He had said, "No, I'm through." Neither money nor anything else could bring him back.

So there was no one in left field or the clean-up slot in the batting order. His retirement left a great big void in an otherwise championship club. And the Sox didn't have anybody ready in the farm system who could hit that long ball to left. No team would trade with them, either. Why should they strengthen the strongest team in the league?

Jug knew he really didn't have a chance of filling the gap, except for this stubborn kid, Mike Jaffe. Mike, he knew by this time, was a mediocre pitcher, barely good enough to get by in the majors. Nevertheless, he did have a lot more to him than mediocrity—though not as a pitcher.

Mike had shown, in his occasional pinch-hitting assignments during his required two years on the Blue Sox bench, that he could belt that long one to left—that real long-gone one. He had a natural batting eye, a powerful swoop when he swung a bat, an easy grace, and beautiful timing. He had big shoulders and strong wrists. *And* youth.

"Never mind," Jug said to him. "Forget I ever mentioned it."

"I will, Mr. Slavin," Mike Jaffe said.

CHAPTER

2

OUT on the field the final intrasquad game of the training season was about to begin. Today was the end of phase one in the spring grind. Phase two, the exhibition schedule with other clubs who had pitched their camps in Florida, would start tomorrow. After this would come the rest of the exhibition games on the long zigzagging path home. Jug Slavin was thinking that, unlike the rest of the league, the Blue Sox had a starting line-up which was almost set right now. All he lacked was an authentic clean-up hitter, which was, he told himself ruefully, the same as saying an airplane had everything except a propeller.

Jug sat down in the dugout and gazed across the ball park. The infield looked a glaring white in the bright, hot Florida sun. The outfield was as hard and dry as the one at the Stadium would be in late August. The small grandstand was about one-third full, dotted with sport shirts and T shirts and gay, colored dresses. Mike Jaffe was showing a small boy in a front-row seat how to grip a curve ball. Mike, Jug knew, was working on a slider this spring, because his three-year pro record as a pitcher indicated that something drastic must be done.

The Tillmans were playing the Murphys today, a six-inning contest. Coach Tweet Tillman's line-up was made up entirely of the regulars; Coach Fido Murphy's bunch were called the Yannigans. Jug had arranged it that way. Every man on the Tillman squad was bonded championship stuff, with one exception—Sonny Bellucci in left field. Bellucci had hit .340 in Double-A last year, but Jug doubted that he would hit .240 in this league. Yet Bellucci was his outstanding candidate to replace Kennie Willard.

Warm-up tosses were now being thrown by Eddie Lasky into the big, waiting mitt of Pete Gibbs, the rangiest and best-hitting catcher in the league. Lasky had missed the twenty-game mark just once in the past six years, and last season he had won twenty-three while losing nine.

At first base was Stretch Stookey, who, a few years ago, had been just a tall toothpick of a kid but had now filled out into the muscled proportions of a trim light-heavyweight fighter. Stretch bounced the dirty infield-practice ball to Bud Walker at second. That incredibly fast man on a pivot scooped it and snapped it back to Stookey in practically the same motion. Walker could do just about anything with a hard hopper except dribble it like a basketball player.

Standing at shortstop, hands on hips, was Handy Andy Pearson, otherwise known as this league's Mister Shortstop. Andy was watching the preliminary unveiling of Lasky with as much intentness as if this was going to be an official game back home at Blue Sox Stadium. Stookey yelled at him to pay attention as he bounced the practice ball across the infield. Andy reached down and gloved it, then tossed a strike back to Stookey.

Johnny Madigan, at third, was ready and waiting when the ball came his way. He dove at it and rifled it back. Even this early, Madigan couldn't take things easy; he didn't know how to take things easy. That was probably the reason why, after ten years, he still rated the hard-earned title of peskiest lead-off man around. Madigan was small, as Blue

Soxers went; he had never hit .300 in his life; he had come up from the minors tagged "good field, no hit"; and he had still been on the All-Star team last year.

Jug's gaze shifted to right field. Waiting there, pounding his right fist into his glove with the impatience of a sand-lotter, was Chip Fiske, the smallest man on the team. He was a hit-and-run artist, whose highest home-run total for a season was three, but his chip-shot singles and doubles had enabled him to average better than two hundred hits every season since he had come up. And he had an arm that base runners did not challenge often.

But in center field stood the prize Blue Sox package of them all—Russ Woodward, the switch-hitting powerhouse. Woodward, Jug figured, would have to be his clean-up man as matters stood now. The trouble with that arrangement, in Jug's eyes, was that Woodward belonged where he had been hitting, in the third-place slot. If intentional walks were pitchers' compliments, then Woodward could truly feel almost flattered to death; and without a solid threat batting after him, he would find himself being waved to first base every time he turned around. Woodward was a born center fielder. He had the speed, the instinct for getting the jump on the ball, and the height to trap some of the long ones in the webbing of his glove just as they were about to fall into the bleachers.

Reluctantly, Jug turned his eyes to left field. Sonny Bellucci had been in the Sox farm system for five years, and the reports on him said that although he could murder a ball when he got what he wanted, he could be pitched to. His strike-out total always overshadowed his extra-base totals. From observation this spring Jug knew that once he had been around the league, the pitchers with control would manipulate Bellucci as easily as if he were a toy monkey-on-a-stick. And batting coaches, so far, had been at a loss to solve his problem.

As Lasky made his final warm-up toss and Gibbs threw the ball down to Pearson, who was standing on the second-base bag, Stan Davis came into the dugout and sat down beside Jug. Davis was the general manager. When the farm system failed to produce an adequate replacement for a faded veteran, he received the blame. He was a man who could carry on a rapid-fire conversation and still miss nothing that was going on around him.

He didn't look at Jug as he spoke, just kept staring out at the field. "You talked to the kid?"

"Just now," Jug said.

"And?"

"He thinks the Babe made a great mistake when he quit pitching."

Davis turned his eyes from the field for a moment and looked right at Jug. "Listen," he said. "I'll talk to this boy. What kind of a twenty-year-old fool is he? Here's a chance to be in a World Series instead of finishing out the season pitching for Potsdam—" He broke off as Mike Jaffe walked by.

Jug called to him. "Mike, you pitch the middle two innings for the Murphys. So get yourself ready." Mike nodded and kept going. Jug turned to Stan Davis and said, "Don't you talk to him yet, Stan. Let me handle this thing for a while."

"You're babying him."

"I'm figuring," Jug said, "that in Mike Jaffe we've not only got a sixty-thousand-dollar investment, but maybe we've got a future Williams, Mantle, DiMag. He can hit a baseball as well as that."

"I've seen it."

"But if he converts under orders—under threats—it won't work. He's got to do it willingly. Give me time."

"How much time?"

"Until we get north."

"Meanwhile Bellucci—"

"Bellucci won't do," Jug said. "I know that right

now. Meanwhile, I'll make Jaffe shag fly balls every day, just to strengthen his legs for his pitching, see?"

"Well, all right then. What about hitting practice?"

"That's a cinch," Jug said. "I'll tell him I'm counting on him as my number one right-handed pinch hitter, that it'll mean he's that much more valuable to the team. He'll go along with that. And by the time we get north, he'll have been chasing flies and hitting just about ten times as much as he'll have been pitching. I'll see to that."

Davis put a restraining hand on Jug's knee. "Quiet," he said. "Here comes the sixty-thousand-dollar slob now."

CHAPTER
3

WHAT had bothered Mike Jaffe most last year had been the fans' applause. The trouble was that from his point of view, it had always come at the wrong time. He had spent the season with the Sox' Triple-A farm team, the Blues, after sweating out his two years as a bonus boy on the Sox bench. The applause had almost never come when his name was announced over the loud-speaker system as the starting pitcher; it had always come when he was announced as a pinch hitter in a crucial late-inning spot.

It was funny, in a way. Most pitchers liked to talk about their hitting. When they managed to get a couple of hits they talked of them, even if they had pitched a shutout. With Mike it was different. He got more than his share of hits, and toward the end of the season, when he pitched a ball game he sometimes batted seventh in the order if the other pitcher was left-handed. When teammates or fans paid him a compliment, it had always been about his hitting, never about his pitching.

His pitching hadn't been bad. He had won twelve and lost fourteen, and for his first year in Triple-A that certainly showed he had something on the ball. Of course, it wasn't quite as impressive as his high-school record, which had caused all the ruckus among the scouts who had wanted to sign him. That last year in high school he hadn't lost a game, and he had pitched six shutouts and three no-hitters. Pro ball was different; the hitters were pretty smart even in Triple-A. But he had no doubt about his ability to make the big time. Perhaps if his batting average hadn't been so much better than his earned-run average, players wouldn't have held back so much in talking about the stuff he threw. All he knew was that he had spent too many years learning to pitch, thinking of himself as a pitcher, to get much kick out of just hearing people say nice things about the way he swung a bat.

His father had been the one who believed completely in him as a pitcher, and he had never paid much attention to his hitting. Whatever Mike seemed to know about hitting must have come naturally, because he had gone through the motions with no more enthusiasm than he had felt when performing calisthenics. It had been Big Ed Jaffe's dream, ever since Mike could remember, that his son would be a big-league pitcher. Big Ed Jaffe had never been able to make it, even though he had spent a baseball lifetime pitching in the minors. Once he'd had a spring-training trial with the Blue Sox, but it had been brief. He had worked with Mike, year after year, catching for him in the back yard, going to all his games from the Little League on up. He hadn't lived long enough to see Mike's great senior year in high school or to see the big-league scouts fight over him. In the end, Mike had picked the Blue Sox, because they had been the only big-league club to give his father at least a quick look in the spring.

Mike felt now that if he didn't do everything he could to fulfill the ambition his father had cherished for him and had worked so hard to help him achieve, he would be letting him down. Besides, he liked to pitch, liked to whip that fast ball in there, liked the feeling of supreme self-reliance that only a pitcher could know, out there on the mound.

Everything was up to him, one man against nine. Mike guessed that an airplane pilot got the same feeling when he was alone in the clouds and all on his own.

Mike knew, when he went out to pitch the middle two innings for the Yannigans against the Regulars, that he was being talked about in the dugout. He had sensed, when he had walked by the dugout and seen Stan Davis, the general manager, there with Jug, that the subject of his refusal to give up pitching and convert to the outfield had probably come up. He was glad that he had settled it, once and for all, with Jug. Now it was up to him to show that he was too valuable as a pitcher to fool around in left field.

The first batter he faced in the bottom of the third was Chip Fiske. Willie (the Lion) Simms was his catcher, and Willie called for the curve. Surprisingly enough, the Yannigans had a 2 to 1 lead, and Mike wanted to hold it as badly as if this had been an official game against the Clippers, with first place at stake.

Mike's curve ball missed and Fiske just waited, not even moving his body. He threw the fast one, low, but it missed the corner and Fiske refused to go after it. This time Mike almost aimed the ball, and he knew as soon as it left his hand that aiming the ball would bring, as always, bad news. It did. Fiske swung and the ball streaked between right and center. It kept on rolling and Fiske, to whom a double was a long blow, wound up on third base.

Now Woodward stepped in, batting left-handed against Mike. Woodward picked off the first pitch, even though it was high and probably would have been a ball. It was slammed, not hit, to dead center, and there was no question about its going for extra bases unless a miracle occurred far out in the field. The center fielder, up from Albany for a look, was no miracle man. The ball caromed off the base of the fence in deepest left center, and before anybody could catch up with it and relay it in, Woodward was across the plate with an inside-the-park home run.

Tillmans 3 now, Murphys 2.

Willie the Lion walked out to the mound, his left arm crooked so that his mitt was shoved against his bulging waist. "Trouble is," the Lion said, "you're aimin' that ball, man."

"I know," Mike said.

"Don't worry about a walk. Too early in the season to worry about that."

Mike nodded.

"Just pitch to me," the Lion said, as he turned and walked back to the plate.

Mike just pitched to him and he got Stretch Stookey, who was batting clean-up today, on a long hoist to right. But he knew he'd been lucky, for the wind was blowing from right field.

Pete Gibbs walked. Andy Pearson dumped a humpbacked single into left, Gibbs holding at second. But Walker grounded sharply to first and both men advanced. Then the only rookie in the line-up, Sonny Bellucci, stepped in.

Bellucci batted right-handed and took the kind of toe hold in the box that almost challenged a pitcher to brush him back with a high hard one. Mike knew Bellucci had power but couldn't do much with a ball thrown low and away when it nicked the corner.

Mike tried, three times, to give Bellucci just that. But he missed every time and Bellucci didn't bite. Then he came in with one, aiming again, and Bellucci had the hit sign, of course, because Slavin wanted to see him hit, not walk, if possible. Bellucci hit. It went high and deep, far to left. There was no doubt it was out of the lot, but there was doubt that it would stay fair. It did, by just a foot or two, and three more runs jogged across the plate.

[25]

He struck out Lasky, after running the count to three and two, and walked into the dugout with the Yannigans now trailing, 2 to 6.

As it turned out, he was the second man to bat in the inning. The lead-off man flied out. Mike walked up to the plate, not swinging any bats, just dragging one bat after him. He looked like anything except a hitter until he got set for the pitch. Then, instinctively, his big frame went into a slight crouch. The bat came back, even with his shoulders. He had a good, loose look about his stance, a stance that he seemed to fall into without thinking.

Mike watched a ball and a strike go by and then he swung. The ball was blasted to left field, but deep left field, and out toward center. It wasn't high. It was a line drive which seemed to rise and rise and finally it, too, disappeared from sight.

When he came in to the bench, Jug said, "It looked sweet, kid. Better hit the showers. I want to experiment with a little left-hander from Scranton who's all warmed up."

Mike shrugged and headed for the rickety clubhouse. He felt no glow from the long, solid blast he'd given the ball. His mind was too busy dwelling on the fact that he'd given up five runs, two of them homers, and that he hadn't looked very good to the general manager, Stan Davis.

Inside the clubhouse he was joined by Lasky, who had also left the game. "Nice blow, kid," Lasky said. "You seem to hit 'em wherever they're thrown —high, low, or across the belt. That was a high one, wasn't it?"

"I didn't especially notice," Mike said.

"It traveled a lot more than four hundred feet," Lasky went on.

Mike shrugged. "I had the wind with me," he said.

CHAPTER
4

MIKE wasn't too surprised to find that Jug worked him pretty hard through the exhibition campaign that followed. Jug didn't pitch him so often, since he was more interested in getting a line on a number of others who were not as sure to stick with the Sox as Mike was; but Jug insisted that he put in a lot of time shagging flies in practice and taking as many batting-practice cuts at the ball as the regulars. That was O.K. with Mike. At twenty he was by far the youngest of the group who would comprise the squad on opening day—he was sure he would be in that group—and he could use the work.

"Get your legs as strong as you can," Jug said. "Nothing is better for strengthening them than shagging flies every day."

Mike agreed.

"And take full batting practice every day," Jug said. "Remember, I expect you'll be my number one right-handed pinch hitter."

Mike nodded vigorously.

"It might even turn out," Jug said, "that if we had serious outfield injuries, you could fill in in a pinch, which would make you twice as valuable to the club."

"I'll go all out on anything you say," Mike assured him. "Just so long as it doesn't interfere with my pitching."

"Fine," Jug said. "Now today Bellucci's got a pulled muscle. You pitched three innings day before yesterday, so I won't use you. Suppose you put in a little time in left field, just to get used to it in a real game."

"My arm feels all right. I could pitch a few innings."

"I want to try out some unknown material," Jug said. "And Lasky wants to go three. He paces himself down here, and he knows best, at his age, just when he ought to go."

"All right," Mike said. "I'll fill in for Bellucci."

"Fine," Jug said. "You'll bat fourth."

"Clean-up! *Me?*"

"You," Jug said, and walked away.

Mike felt immensely flattered that Jug was batting him clean-up, right behind Russ Woodward, but it didn't make too much sense to him. After all, he was just a sometimes hitter. He knew he could rock that ball when he really got hold of one. He remembered in high school that even though he had always pitched, the coach had still batted him clean-up. That had been in high school, however, and now he was in the big leagues. There was a great difference, and his guess was he wouldn't even hit .250 against big-league pitching. He knew, because, after all, he was a big-league pitcher himself. In his own mind, at least, he was established as one.

The Sox were playing the Redskins today. In the first inning Madigan took a called third strike while trying fiercely to work the pitcher for a walk. But Chip Fiske slashed a single to right and Russ Woodward disdained a three-and-two pitch that was inches wide, so he strolled to first and Fiske to second.

When Mike stepped in, he looked down the third-base line for the sign from Tweet Tillman. There wasn't any. He was free to do what he wanted to.

He took a strike and then two balls. He could sense the way the next one would come in, even before he saw the ball leave the pitcher's hand. He guessed right, and when he came around on it he came around all the way. It left his bat, as baseballs so often did, on a level line; but this one didn't rise. It went right at the third baseman, with such force that even though he gloved it, it literally knocked him over, flat on his back. But he held onto it, because he was unable to try for a double play from that position.

In the dugout, Jug said, "I've seen hard-hit drives, but I never before saw one hit that hard."

"Just an out," Mike said.

"Yeah," Jug said. "Just an out."

Next time up, Mike fouled two out of the park, down the left-field line, both missing the home-run zone by only a foot or two. Then he went down swinging.

Finally, in his third trip to the plate, he connected. There were men on first and third, and his line drive kept rising, as it usually did. It rose beyond the outstretched glove of the leaping Redskin left fielder and crashed the fence. Mike wound up with a double, and two runners came across the plate.

Jug took him out then, saying he'd had enough for the day. He had caught two routine fly balls and had been waved away from another, tougher one, in left center, by Woodward.

In the dressing room later, Woodward started to talk to him. "Mike," he said, "who told you you were a pitcher?"

"My father," Mike said.

"Oh," Woodward said thoughtfully.

"I pitched three no-hitters my last year in high school," Mike said, making no attempt to sound casual, letting the pride in his voice come through.

"Well, that's . . . quite a feat," Woodward said. "But you know something about yourself?"

"What?"

"You can hit a baseball just about as hard as I can, and they say I can hit one just about as hard as the next guy."

"I don't know anything about hitting," Mike said. "I never studied it. My father only taught me pitching."

"You never studied hitting," Woodward said, "any more than a bird ever studied flying."

"What do you mean by that?"

"Figure it out," Woodward said, as he headed toward the shower.

In a way it baffled Mike that everybody kept complimenting him on his hitting, when he really didn't know what he was doing up there at the plate. He just went up, hoping he would outguess the pitcher, and sometimes he got hold of one. But nobody, not a single soul, had said a kind word about his pitching since he had reached the Blue Sox camp. His hitting was a fluke; his pitching was a talent carefully tutored. In ten years he would be the best pitcher in the league, or close to it. But in the same ten years he would be just another hitter who, once in a while, connected for the long ball.

His father had said, "Once you get big-league control and big-league poise, there'll be no stopping you. The only person who can stop you from being a great pitcher is yourself. Always believe in that arm and that head that you've got."

Thinking back, Mike couldn't remember his father's ever saying a single word about his hitting.

A funny thing happened in New Orleans. By this time the Sox had broken camp and had started the twisting trip that would eventually land them at the Stadium by the middle of April. In this game, which Mike sat out, Jug sent him to pinch-hit for Bix Hanson, the pitcher, in the top of the seventh. The Sox were behind the minor-league Pelicans, 4 to 6. Pearson was on third and Walker was on second. There were two outs.

The minute Mike stepped into the box, the Pelican catcher stepped off to the side. For the first time since he had been with the Blue Sox, Mike realized he was being given an intentional pass. The Pelicans didn't want to pitch to him in this spot. It wasn't just because the Pelican pitcher was left-handed; after all, Madigan followed, and Madigan batted right-handed too.

Mike could hardly believe it. They preferred to pitch to Madigan, the old pro, rather than to Mike Jaffe, a rookie pitcher. They weren't setting up a double play, either, because there were two outs. They must have thought that Madigan was less dangerous than Mike Jaffe. He trotted to first base, feeling embarrassed for Madigan.

He need not have. Madigan promptly shoved the insult down their throats. He clipped one of his patented seeing-eye singles, a trickling grounder that moved unhurriedly toward right field, just beyond the frantic clutches of the Pelican first baseman and the Pelican second baseman. It was good for two runs and tied the score. Then Fiske doubled, Woodward walked, and Stookey cleaned the bases with another double.

Mike couldn't get over it, but Madigan could. Madigan said to him, "Well, Mike, the word has got around. Even the Pelicans know you're on the way up and I'm on the way down."

"You showed 'em, Johnny," Mike said.

"I'll still show 'em when I'm in the casket," Madigan said. "But they made the right move. You've got yourself a reputation, kid—even this early in the spring. They know you're a hitter."

"I'm a pitcher," Mike said.

"Sure, sure," Madigan said. "But they don't know that yet. All they know is, you can whale a baseball."

CHAPTER
5

IT WASN'T until the team reached Baltimore on the trip north that Mike stopped to realize he'd been playing left field a lot more than he'd been pitching. Also it dawned on him that Fido Murphy, who'd been an outfielder back when Ty Cobb had gone into second with his spikes high, had been giving him a lot of casual, friendly advice about playing the position. Not only that, but Russ Woodward and Chip Fiske kept talking to him in the clubhouse, on the bench, even during movies, about this little thing and that in the daily life of an outfielder. Nobody, absolutely nobody, had talked to him about pitching.

In Baltimore Bellucci left the team to head for

the Rochester spring-training camp. Mike knew, everybody knew, that Bellucci had blown it. There was nobody left to fill Kennie Willard's place except a couple of farm hands whose names Mike could never quite remember. It was in Baltimore that Mike suddenly realized he was not getting anywhere as a pitcher with the Sox, but that a big fuss was being made over him by almost everyone as a hitter and as a left fielder. This was when he decided that a trap had been set and that he was falling into it.

Mike went to Jug. "I haven't pitched an inning for five days," he said. "When do I pitch next?"

"Well," Jug said, "I got this certain rotation set. I hate to break it up. . . ."

"My arm needs work," Mike told him.

"Look, son," Jug said, "I'll give it to you straight. You don't figure in my pitching plans. To be blunt, pitchers like you can stick around, move from this team to that, but you come a dime a dozen."

"Thanks," Mike said. "Thanks a lot, Mr. Slavin."

"What do you want me to do?" Jug demanded. "Kid you along?"

"Then why am I still with the team? Others have gone. Bellucci, that Carlson. . . ."

"Don't you really know why you're still with us?" Jug asked.

"I guess I do," Mike said. "Hitting."

"You are so correct," Jug said. "You can stick with this club, Mike. You can be in the starting line-up. If, and it's a great big if, you get your heart into doing what comes naturally to you—hitting."

"I told you," Mike said, "way back in the beginning. I'm a pitcher. My father—"

"Michael Jaffe," Jug said, "I hate to put words into the mouth of a man who is no longer with us, but if your father were still here and saw what I see, what the whole team sees, he would tell you to forget about pitching. He would tell you to convert."

"No he wouldn't," Mike said. "He never would."

"All right," Jug said. "You'll pitch this afternoon. You'll start. Go get yourself warmed up."

Long before game time, Mike sat on the bench with Jug while Baltimore took batting practice. This was a ritual with Jug: the pitcher always sat beside him, and the two of them studied the enemy hitters and made comments about them and got their thinking up to date about each one.

"See that guy?" Jug said. "See what he does with an inside pitch? He drills it every time."

Mike nodded.

"He's bush on the low ball," Jug said.

"It's hard to get the low ball over," Mike said. "That's the toughest."

"That's why relief pitchers were born," Jug said. "But you'd better learn."

A reporter dropped into the dugout and sat down beside them. "Who pitches today, Skip?"

Jug jerked his thumb toward Mike.

"What!" the reporter said. "A left fielder pitching? What is this, anyway—American Legion ball?"

"Never you mind," Jug said.

The reporter looked at Mike and tapped his arm. "A boy hits like this one and you pitch him . . . well. . . ."

Mike said nothing. As the reporter left, Stan Davis came in and sat down next to Mike. Davis said to Jug, "Tell you what, Jughead. I can get you Luke Bates, as fine a left fielder as there ever was. And he hits that long ball to left."

"Used to hit it," Jug said. "How old is he?"

"A young thirty-nine," Davis said. "Batted .328 in the Association last year. Hit twenty-four home runs."

"How long ago was it the Clippers let him go?"

"Only two years," Davis said cheerfully. "He's what you call rejuvenated."

"Umm. . . ." Jug said. "Hold off a while."

"Hold off?" Davis said. "That's a miserable remark for a manager with no clean-up hitter and the season a week away."

"Get good and lost, Mr. Davis," Jug said.

Mike went to the water cooler. He had a feeling the conversation had been rigged up for his benefit. He would show them today. He had no desire to be a left fielder, so how could he possibly be a good one? He had all the desire in the world to be a pitcher, so how could he miss?

There was a certain air of indifference, Mike felt, about seven of the eight men playing behind him that day. It wasn't that any errors were committed; it was more a lack of hustle, a lack of chatter in the infield, an absence of encouraging words. The only player out there who didn't reflect this attitude was Bob Blossom in left field. Now that Jug had given up on Bellucci, Blossom was top candidate for the job. Blossom was a good ballplayer who could hit for an acceptable average and could run and throw. But he couldn't hit that long ball, except once in a while. Still, he was the man most likely to open the season in left, and he was going all out to prove that he belonged there.

In the first inning Blossom barely missed crashing into the wall, as he grabbed a long drive that Mike had thought was really gone when it left the bat. The hitter had been the lead-off man, and immediately Pete Gibbs walked out to the mound to talk.

Pete looked at Mike in a dubious and disapproving manner. "You're still aiming the ball, kid," he said. "As soon as you get behind the hitter you aim."

"I'll quit aiming, Pete," Mike said. He hadn't realized before how much out of the groove a pitcher could get when he laid off a while. Of course, he hadn't actually laid off; he had *been* laid off, and it was just now dawning on him. Things that he could ordinarily do easily were now quite tough.

Mike found out how true that was when he pitched to the second Baltimore batter. He got two strikes on him. Then Pete Gibbs flashed him the next signal and made sure of it by putting his glove on the outside corner of the plate, and low. That was exactly where Mike tried to put the ball. Instead, it went pumping right down the middle, and when the batter hit it, Mike didn't even turn his head. He knew it was gone, knew it was out of the park.

He remembered, as he scuffed the rubber and involuntarily let his head droop, that even when he had been working regularly he sometimes missed with that same pitch. That corner was not too easy to catch. But the count had been two and two; there had been no need to worry about missing the plate. He would have had another shot at it. But still the ball had gone down the middle, down the drain.

All of a sudden Mike's arm didn't feel good. There was a slight twinge, just slight, but still a twinge. He paused, after getting Gibbs's signal, before going into his motion. He was thinking how, out of fear, he'd been experimenting with a slider. And then with a sinker, too. He knew that young pitchers with strong young arms generally stayed with the three basic pitches in this battle against the batters: the fast ball, the curve, and the change-up. Here he was, twenty years old, and he was doing what pitchers usually did at thirty or thirty-two.

He got set to pitch to the third Baltimore hitter, aware now of a tiny throb in his arm. It would be the end, he thought, if he ever let Jug, or anybody, know about that right now. Two men he had faced, and two men had crashed long balls on him. One had been written down on the official scorer's card as an out, but except for the grace and the earnestness of Blossom, it would have been a triple. The other had looked like an eagle in flight.

Now batter number three.

Before Mike went into the pumping motion, he remembered something Eddie Lasky had said to him once. It was disturbing, and particularly so because the remark had come from a man whose pitching prowess was a cornerstone of the Blue Sox pennants, a man who had a bad season if he won only eighteen.

"Slip just a little," Lasky had said, "and people lose their respect. Not just the guys you pitch to or the guys backing you up on the field, but the sports writers and the fans and, most important of all, the front office. It might not be much of a slip. Maybe three straight losses or three home-run balls in a game. But in this business it's enough. The word is passed around. I was fourteen and six for the season once in August, and then I lost two games in a row. I got really nervous, because those Clipper hitters didn't act scared any more. You figure it out."

That speech, a fairly long one for Lasky, was running around inside Mike's head now as he prepared to throw at the third Baltimore hitter. He could see that the hitter was thinking about those two line drives. There was an eager, confident look on this one's face. Mike threw the curve, and he knew,

[43]

the minute it left his hand, that it would hang, and it did. And the Baltimore hitter went after it—the first pitch.

This time he watched the play, and it seemed to him that everything was happening in slow motion. He turned and craned his neck. The ball was headed deep to center, deeper and deeper. Woodward was agile and he was quick, but he could not catch up with this one. He gave it everything—the whole park could see that—but the ball was just too well tagged. It shot over his head, to his right, and banged against a wall there. The runner wound up on third base, despite a fine throw and a fine relay. He slid, but he hadn't really needed to slide. Mike saw Jug walking out toward the mound with Pete Gibbs.

"It's not your day, son," Jug said. He held up his left hand and snapped it down like a salute. Out of the distant bull pen Phil Doyle appeared. Doyle was the compact little guy who had saved more ball games for the Sox than the other seven teams in the league cared to remember.

"Listen," Pete said, "is your arm feeling O.K.? I mean, no kidding, there was nothing on that ball."

"My arm's all right," Mike said.

The three of them stood there silently, until Doyle

reached the mound. Mike tossed him the ball. "It's all yours," Mike said, and he headed toward the dugout and the showers. He knew he'd had it, for that day anyway.

CHAPTER

6

THEY hit the Stadium finally. It was no new place to Mike. He had spent two bonus years here, and it practically felt like home to him. Rookies were awed by it, but he was twenty and no rookie. He took everything in stride.

They had a two-game exhibition series with the Robins, and then they would start to play for the marbles. On the day of the first game with the Robins Mike went to the clubhouse early—so early that no one was there at the time except Pickles, the clubhouse man.

"Hear you been hitting pretty good," Pickles said.

Mike had had enough of these remarks. "I pitched some pretty good innings along the way," he said.

"Not in Baltimore," said Pickles, who was noted for his lack of diplomacy.

"I shut out the Cardinals for three innings in St. Pete," Mike said, wondering why he was suddenly bragging, on the defensive. Actually, he knew why.

"The papers say you can hit that long ball to left," Pickles said. "Matter of fact, I've seen you do it a number of times, when you were here before, when you didn't even shave yet. You shave now, huh?"

Mike nodded. "I think I developed a slider."

"You'll roon your arm with that one, at your tender age," Pickles said.

"Not me," Mike said. "My arm is rugged."

"You'll be using the whirlpool bath real soon if you keep that up, at *your* age."

Mike went over to the sandwich rack, which Pickles always kept loaded. He took a Swiss on rye, and a Coke from the cooler, signing his name on the pad above. The soft drinks cost money, but the sandwiches were on the club.

A reporter strolled in. He was Phil Hamburger, a columnist, Mike remembered, who had written several pieces about him right after he had been signed. Phil wore thick horn-rimmed glasses and was a nosy sort of man, but in a nice way. Phil had never really bothered Mike.

[47]

"You heard about the trade?" Hamburger asked.

"What trade?"

"Davis pulled one off. We got a new pitcher."

"Pitcher!"

"That fast-balling Cuban on the poor Bears. You know the guy, Joe Rodriguez?"

Mike could hardly believe it, but he found himself hoping that he was involved in the deal. With the Sox, World Series or not, he did not stand much of a chance to pitch. With the Bears, the team that had a great season if it finished seventh, he would stand a very good chance.

"Who went?" he asked.

"Not you," Hamburger said. "If that's what you're thinking."

"But who?"

"A bunch of bright young Sox farm hands. The Bears were desperate for a catcher who could hit better than .200, and they got one—Krause from the Blues. If the Sox didn't have two durable guys like Gibbs and the Lion, he'd be here now."

"Who else?"

"Bellucci. The Bears believe in him. And a fine young shortstop from Double-A, not fine enough to worry Pearson, though. It was a good deal for the Bears, even though the Sox didn't have to give up a thing that they needed."

Another front-line pitcher, Mike thought. Rodriguez would be front-line with any team, even the Sox. It looked as if his services as a pitcher were something that the Sox needed even less today than they had needed yesterday.

"The Bears," Hamburger added, "tried to get you instead of Bellucci. But the Sox front office told them you were tagged untouchable."

In a way that was flattering to know, except that when the Sox had acquired Rodriguez they must have come close to writing Mike Jaffe off, for this season at least, as a pitcher. He had a feeling that the front office was going to put the pressure on him in the next couple of days and force him to make a decision that they refused to believe he had already made. They would find out. They could dangle all the bright promises in the world, but they could not manipulate his talents to suit themselves, as they did with most of the other players. It wasn't just the security of all that bonus money he still had in the bank that made him so firm; it was something more important to him than that. He wasn't going to let his father's dreams of almost fifteen years and his father's complete faith in him as a big-league pitcher go by the boards. That just would never happen.

Singly and in pairs the team began to arrive, and the big, cheery clubhouse was soon full of voices, rising and falling. All around him Mike heard comments about the coming of Joe Rodriguez, and the comments were full of enthusiasm. "I could never hit the guy," Fiske was saying to Gibbs. "I'm glad I don't have to bat against him any more. I figure the trade will add ten points to my batting average over a full season."

"He's faster than he looks," Gibbs said, "because he throws with that easy, lazy-looking motion."

The Lion called over, "We'll have lots of nice quiet days out in that bull pen. Got to get me a checkerboard to keep out there."

"On pitching we're set," Madigan said, grinning.

"On everything we're set," Fiske said. "Except in one little place."

"Little, like an ocean."

"It'll get worked out."

Mike stayed out of the conversation. He kept busy, furiously rubbing vaseline into his glove. Then he heard his name called, and when he turned around, Jug was beckoning to him from the door of his office. He stood up, and as he walked across the room he was aware that the big Rodriguez pep rally had suddenly died out and he was being scrutinized from behind.

Jug's office was a neat, businesslike place with a

polished desk and a portable typewriter on top of it, on which Jug wrote reports for later reference after every game. Jug was sitting in the swivel chair behind the desk and Stan Davis was roaming around the room restlessly, pretending to re-examine some of the photographs on the walls. They were pictures of past Blue Sox pennant-winning teams and former great stars who had helped win them: Marty (Beef Trust) Blake, Augie Marshall, Patsy Bates, Vic Valenti, Tommy Shore, and even Tweet Tillman, when he was in his prime as the first-string Sox catcher.

"Sit down, Mike," Jug said, as Davis came over. Davis didn't sit down and didn't even act as though he had any part in this little conference; he behaved more like a casual visitor whose social chat with Jug had been temporarily interrupted. But Mike knew that except for the Sox owner and president, no one else in the whole organization even came close to wielding the final power over a ballplayer's future that Davis did.

"You heard the news, I guess," Jug said.

"The trade? Yes, I did."

"The Bears wanted you instead of Bellucci. We turned them down, of course."

"I don't know why you did," Mike said. "I don't

get the feeling you're going to use me much."

"If you haven't changed your mind," Davis said, "about converting to the outfield the way you were asked to, then you're a very foolish young man."

"I told Mr. Slavin, back in Florida, that I wouldn't quit pitching," Mike said. "I meant it. That was final with me."

"Is that so?" Davis said. He sat down in a chair across the desk from Mike and regarded him with brooding eyes and no sign of a smile on his face. He looked a little like a fighter closing in on his man for the big punch. "Look, son," he said, in anything but a fatherly way, "we've got a staff of starting pitchers that begins with proven performers such as Eddie Lasky, Bix Hanson, Joe Rodriguez, Harry Diefendorf—the best. We've got a bull pen that starts with Phil Doyle and Bernie Glaser. Right now if Bob Feller and Don Newcombe were your age and our property, I doubt if we could make room for them on this staff, this year. I'm not exaggerating, except possibly a little bit."

"If my chances are that hopeless," Mike said, "I think you ought to have traded me when you had the chance."

Davis said, "Two things stopped me from doing it, Jaffe. One is that we've invested considerable money in you. The other is we think you could help solve the only big problem we've got—left field."

"I told Mr. Slavin in Florida—"

"Mike," Jug said, "did I mention to you in Florida that Musial also thought he was a pitcher for several years until somebody discovered that he could hit pretty well?"

"It's no use your trying to talk me out of pitching," Mike said. "My father spent a dozen years teaching me to pitch. He believed in me. So did the Sox, else they wouldn't have paid me that big bonus to sign —as a pitcher."

"We hadn't seen you hit against major-league pitching then," Jug said.

"Tell you what, Jug," Davis said. "We've wasted enough time talking to this lad. Let him have his own way. I can still get Luke Bates from the Association, and we'll get some mileage out of him if Blossom alternates with him out there." He turned to go, his broad back looking rigid and somehow suggesting bottled-up fury. At the door he called back, "See Burt Kelly, the road secretary, Jaffe. Tell him to get you on a train to join the Blues, wherever they are right now. And"—he paused for dramatic effect —"tell him to get you an *upper* berth."

THE manager of the Blues was a spare, elderly man who wore rimless glasses and looked like a soon-to-be-retired high-school teacher. He had had a brief big-league tenure as manager of the Panthers a few years ago, finishing forty-odd games off the pace. When he left he took with him the reputation of being just about the nicest, most considerate guy in the league. Chances were he would never get a second crack at managing in the majors, but the Blue Sox had hired him, because he had a way with young ballplayers. His name was Pops Medlicott.

"Seems kind of unusual," Pops said to Mike, when he reported, "for a twenty-year-old to choose the Blues over the Blue Sox." Pops always had seemed, to Mike, to act slightly puzzled and mildly curious about the off-the-field actions of his younger ballplayers.

"You know the story, don't you, Pops?" Mike said.

"Jug told me on the phone that you didn't want to give the outfield a try."

"They don't think I'm a pitcher up there. You saw me pitch all last season. What did you think?"

Pops blinked behind the glasses. He had the disconcerting habit sometimes of acting as though he hadn't heard a question even when it was point-blank. Mike knew he had, so he waited.

"You did some good pitching for me," Pops said. "You'll help us a lot, just the way you did last year, not only with your arm, but with your bat, too."

"You sound like Jug Slavin."

"That's a high compliment to me, son," Pops said. "He doesn't make many mistakes in sizing up ballplayers. But what I'd give for the chance you turned down. . . . There just isn't anything like being in the big leagues, is there?"

"I'll be there," Mike said. "But when I am I'll be pitching, not shagging flies."

"How soon you ready to pitch?" Pops asked.

"Today."

"Unpack your suitcase. We open the season next

Tuesday. You'll pitch one of the games in the opening series."

Mike had a feeling that Pops had left a lot of things unsaid that had been on the tip of his tongue. Triple-A wasn't the big leagues, but at least you stayed in a fairly good hotel, not a boardinghouse, and you didn't travel by bus. Some of the Blues were fellows he had known last year, a mixture of former big-leaguers fighting for another chance, or definitely on the way down, and kids just a step away from the big chance. When Mike went to the clubhouse he shook hands all around, and while everyone was friendly, he had a feeling that they treated him as someone they couldn't fully understand any more.

Mike remembered the Blues' shortstop, Slick Hammill, in particular. Slick had made a flashy start with the Sox, but Andy Pearson had taken the job away from him by not being flashy, just steady and a team man all the way.

Hammill, at twenty-six, was just about as bitter on the subject of pro ball as it was possible to be at that age. "You're crazy, of course," he said. "But I admire your kind of craziness."

Mike looked baffled. "What's crazy about wanting to be what you know you were cut out to be?"

"Listen to me, my young friend. If you don't already know that those boys upstairs are all mixed up, you'll know it soon." Slick was a wiry man with a boy's face on a full-grown body. He had a hard set to his mouth and a belligerent thrust to his sharp chin. Mike knew, from stories he had been told about Slick, that he could hit and field in major-league style, but that he had an ego and an attitude no manager in the league wanted to tangle with. The Sox had offered to sell him to a half-dozen clubs, but there were no takers.

"I'm not mad at anybody," Mike said, sensing that Slick was mad at just about everyone.

"You will be, you will be," Slick said. "When you're twenty-six like me, and still playing in a bush league, like me, and you know you're better than at least half of them up there . . . you'll be mad."

"I'll get up there again," Mike said.

"They gave me a bum deal; now they give you a bum deal. If you want to quit on yourself—convert, I mean—they'll give you another chance. Otherwise, you're here to stay."

"What did they do to you?" Mike asked.

Slick's whole face turned into one big sneer. "They didn't want me to convert. Just wanted me to change my style of play, change my way of looking at things. And because I stuck to my guns, the way you have so far, I'm still in exile."

"I'll get my chance when I prove myself. Jug Slavin said—"

"Jug Slavin! I wouldn't put him in charge of a bunch of hamsters. Maybe you think you'll wake up one morning and find he's recalled you and has sent Rodriguez down?"

Mike broke the conversation up. He didn't want to keep on talking to Slick Hammill, not just then, anyway. He felt low enough as it was. He watched the Blues take an exhibition game from a Double-A team. He was surprised when Pops Medlicott asked him to pinch-hit in the sixth, for the pitcher. "Just to keep you loose up there," Pops said. "The fans around this town never forgot some of those ball games you broke up with your bat last year."

Mike watched a third strike go by on the two and two count, and he couldn't decide later whether he had been fooled or whether he had let it go by because of the mood he was in.

That night, looking over the local sports page, he saw a fairly long story about his return to the Blues. He didn't feel any better after he had read it.

The best-looking natural hitter the Blues' fans

have seen in a good many years returned to the fold today. Mike Jaffe is back, and by his own choice, too, according to the rumors. Mike also pitches. He had a 12–14 record here last year, which was respectable enough for a first full year, and one a lot of rookies would settle for. But once you've seen Mike swing a bat, you forget he's a pitcher. The story has it that he's back with us lucky people because he refused to convert to the outfield for the Sox. If this is true it's a story that will seem incredible to literally thousands of minor-league ballplayers all over the country. And if Pops Medlicott doesn't make some use of Mike's extraordinary batting eye and power, he'll have a lot of disgruntled fans around these parts. Of course, you can't force a boy to quit pitching when he's got his heart set on doing just that and nothing else, because ballplayers, no matter how richly blessed with talent, can't achieve greatness when the desire isn't there. Mike Jaffe has already demonstrated that he has certain skills as a pitcher; but, let's face it, they're limited ones. As a pitcher he can be impressive upon occasion; as a hitter he can be awesome, even in the process of striking out. In any case, the Blues are fortunate to have him back for an-

LONG BALL TO LEFT FIELD

other season, no matter how unhappy the fans may be because they can only watch him swing a bat every fourth day instead of every day.

Along with the story, Mike saw a picture of himself in action in a game last year. He stared at it and frowned. The picture didn't show him on the mound, throwing at a hitter; it showed him in the batter's box, hitting at a pitcher.

CHAPTER

8

THE BLUES' park held eighteen thousand people when it was completely full, but that hadn't happened in the last ten years. It happened on this opening day though, and there was no question about what had caused this pleasant phenomenon —Mike Jaffe.

Pops Medlicott had announced days earlier that Mike would not only pitch the opener, he would bat in the clean-up spot. Managers before Pops had batted good hitting pitchers other places than ninth in the order, but never in clean-up. Pops explained the move merely by saying, "He'll be my best power hitter in the line-up. I'd be a fool to bat him anywhere else, wouldn't I?"

Apparently the capacity crowd agreed. When

Mike heard his name announced over the loud-speaker system, " . . . pitching *and* hitting fourth, Mike Jaffe," the roar from the stands couldn't have been louder if the announcement had been to the effect that Mickey Mantle had been optioned to the Blues.

At the time Mike was completing his pregame warm-up on the first-base side of home plate, fairly near the front-row boxes. As soon as the yelling died down, even while the rest of the batting order was being announced, fans were calling to him.

"Four or five long ones to left today, Mike!"

"Swing from the heels, Mike!"

"So we finally got a clean-up hitter on this club!"

"Swing away, Mike!"

He tossed his last pitch and headed for the dug-out, waving his glove at them in a friendly fashion. But he didn't feel pleased, not at all. Even here he was not getting the slightest sign of acceptance as a pitcher, just as a hitter. He was right back where he had been in Jug Slavin's office when Stan Davis had told him to take off.

Inside the dugout, Bob Cosier, who batted third, said to him, "No walks for me today. Not with you following."

Mike grunted.

Slick Hammill gave him his wise, knowing grin. He knew what Mike was thinking about, and proved it when he said, out of the side of his mouth, "Well, we're right back where we started—on the sand lots. Pitcher hits clean-up today, pitcher plays left field tomorrow."

"Not me," Mike said.

"Want to bet?" Slick said, with a half-snicker.

Mike went to the water cooler and rinsed his mouth.

Pops Medlicott came over and pointed to the stands. "See this crowd?" he said. "People don't jam ball parks any more to watch a pitcher pitch. They jam them to watch a hitter hit. That's why sluggers seldom die broke."

Mike didn't answer.

He felt tensed up, from the first pitch, and he walked the lead-off man. The second one bunted, to the left of the mound. Mike started slow, grabbed in haste, dropped the ball, and then didn't throw to first at all, because he was just too late. The first baseman of the Blues walked over, Carl Perutz.

Perutz looked about as cheering as a barometer during the onrush of a hurricane. "I wouldn't worry about it," he said.

Bob Cosier arrived from third base. "Don't let

it bother you," he said, looking just about as bothered as Perutz, and glancing toward the bull pen.

They went back to their positions. Mike saw Pops Medlicott get off his seat in the dugout and stand with one foot on the bottom step. Then, four times in a row, Mike tried to keep it low, and he did—too low, too wide. The bases were loaded, nobody out, and Pops Medlicott was on his way to the mound. The crowd began to boo Medlicott.

"Leave him alone!"

"Let him get a chance to hit!"

"We want Jaffe!"

"Stay in there, Mike boy!"

Medlicott said, "Slow down a little, Mike. You're working a little fast. Your stuff looks good."

The runners on the bases didn't bother Mike, not too much anyway. What bothered him was the feeling that the fans were treating him like something of a freak. They didn't care about his pitching; they were willing to go along with a bad pitching performance as long as they could see him hit. He felt like an actor whose audience didn't care how badly he acted as long as they could admire his handsome appearance. There wasn't much satisfaction in it.

Now the clean-up hitter dug in. Mike threw the

fast one and the batter let it go by, for a called strike. He protested and Mike thought the hitter was probably right and the umpire wrong, but he felt thankful for the break. He threw the change-up and it was a wrong guess. The hitter swung. The ball shot back on a line just over his head and out of reach into dead center, for a two-run single. The runner on first reached third.

Mike's catcher came out to talk to him and the crowd booed the catcher. The next hitter banged a long fly to right center and the third run came in. The next one doubled, driving in the fourth run, but he was out trying to stretch the hit into a triple. The final out was another line-drive shot, which Slick Hammill managed to glove by diving sideways. Walking off the mound, Mike knew he had been lucky to get out of the inning with only four runs. The crowd applauded him as he approached the dugout, but he couldn't tip his hat. The applause was a joke, even though the crowd didn't mean it that way.

The Blues started their half of the inning, every one of them swinging. Hammill led off with a triple to deep right center. Perutz singled him home. Cosier slapped an outside pitch into right field, good for a soft single that sent Perutz to third. Mike, who had stayed inside the dugout instead of waiting in the on-deck circle, headed toward the plate, grasping just a single bat and moving slowly, as pitchers often do. He was startled to find himself getting a standing ovation from the crowd. He had just pitched the poorest first inning he ever hoped to commit, and despite this the thousands of fans actually stood up to applaud him.

He assumed his natural stance, a deceptively casual and almost lazy-looking one. There seemed to be no rigidity in his body; he appeared as loose as a man who is doing something merely for the fun of it.

A wide pitch went by for ball one. The second one was to his liking, and he ripped it on a line, past third base but foul. It crashed against the retaining wall along the left-field seats. One and one. Two more balls went by. He looked down the third-base line to the Blues' coach and saw he had the hit sign on the three-and-one pitch. The next ball wasn't the best one he had ever swung at; it was too high and tight. But with a fierce desire that surprised him, he wanted to avoid a walk, so he came around on it.

This one was a line drive too, and it went straight down the third-base line. But unlike the first one, it stayed inside the foul line—just by inches, but inside. It shot deep into the corner, where the left fielder scrambled for it. Perutz crossed the plate, Cosier followed him, and Mike wound up on second. The score was 4 to 3 now, and nobody out.

It took a ground-out and a sacrifice fly to bring Mike in with the tying run. That was all for the inning, but he went back to the mound all even with the opposition once more.

It was that kind of game all the way, a seesaw affair, with runs pouring across in clusters for both sides. The Blues finally took it, 13 to 11. The opposition used five pitchers; the Blues used one—Mike Jaffe. For the day he collected a double, a triple, and three walks in six times at bat.

When Mike left the field, the crowd was still cheering him as they filed out. The noise meant almost nothing to him, though; he had never felt less like a pitcher in his life. Well, he would make up for this miserable performance next time out. In his opinion, Pops Medlicott had had no business leaving him in on a day when he didn't have his stuff. Winning meant nothing when you won by a score of 13 to 11. That is, it meant nothing when you were a pitcher.

CHAPTER

9

IT TOOK a full month with the Blues to show Mike that it was the same old story, last year all over again. The fans accepted him as a pitcher, in a lukewarm way; but they practically idolized him as a hitter. His pitching record showed three won and four lost. His batting average, which included a pinch-hitting chore almost every time the Blues were behind in the late innings, was .348.

Mike kept close track of what the Blue Sox were doing. They weren't off to a good start—fourth place after five weeks. Jug seemed to be changing his batting order, through the middle, at least once a week. At first, when Luke Bates played, he batted clean-up. When Bob Blossom went in to rest him, Blossom batted seventh and Stretch Stookey batted clean-up. Then Stookey was switched to batting third, Russ Woodward to clean-up, and Bates to fifth. Next Woodward was put back where he belonged, in the third spot, and Pete Gibbs was tried at clean-up. No Blue Sox team of recent years had resorted to so much juggling of its batting order, the papers pointed out.

Their pitching was good, but that lack of run-driving-in punch through the middle of the order was putting pressure on them. The Sox hadn't yet had a single big inning this season. Three runs were the most they had scored in one inning so far. Rodriguez had won just one game, but he had lost others by 3-2, 4-1, and 2-0. He had actually been pitching great ball.

Pops Medlicott came to Mike one day and made the inevitable remark, the one Mike had known he was bound to make sooner or later. "Son," he said, "I want you to start in left field for us today. The team needs that bat of yours."

"If I do it once I'll be doing it a lot," Mike said. "Then what will happen to my pitching rotation?"

"Your pitching rotation, to be honest, Mike, isn't nearly as important to this club as your hitting is. Last time I looked, your average was over .340. And you had almost as many extra-base hits as singles."

"Somebody put you up to this," Mike said. "Somebody in the front office."

"What if they did?" Pops said. "You've been willing to play left field in batting practice, polishing up on the fly chasing. Why won't you do it in a game?"

"I shagged flies so in case somebody got hurt, I could help out, in a pinch."

"Nobody got hurt," Pops said. "But this is a pinch just the same. We're in sixth place."

"Nobody can make me quit pitching."

"Well, I hate to bring this up," Pops said. "But it's orders from the front office. They said if you still refused, there was nothing to do but tell you the truth. You're a Triple-A hitter, but you're not a Triple-A pitcher. Not yet, anyway."

"Meaning?"

"They want to send me some pitching help, and they've got it to send. If you won't convert, the orders are you're to be dropped to Double-A to make room for somebody new on the staff who can help us climb out of sixth place and into the first division."

Mike turned his head quickly, as though he had been slapped. Suddenly Slick Hammill's bitter words came back to him, the words he had heard from Hammill the day of his arrival at the Blues' camp. "I'm not mad at anybody," he remembered saying to Hammill. And Hammill had replied, "You will be, you will be. When you're twenty-six like me, and still playing in a bush league, like me, and you know you're better than half of them up there, you'll be mad."

Well, Hammill had been right. Now Mike *was* mad, and he wasn't twenty-six yet, either. The thought of being dropped from the big leagues to Triple-A, and now to Double-A, all in a matter of weeks, made him feel sick. And it was just possible they would keep on dropping him down until he gave in to their orders and converted. He had heard all about the lower minors: nothing but night games, long bus rides, bum food, living in furnished rooms —all the tough part of pro ball that he had been lucky enough to escape so far.

This was it. He could stick to pitching and get prepared to face all that, probably before this season was over. Or he could convert to left field, as they were trying to force him to do, and probably he would be back with the Sox soon. He could live in the way he had grown accustomed to, and become part of the only world that mattered in all baseball players' minds.

Mike finally forced himself to look Pops Medlicott in the eye again. "*You* don't want me as a pitcher, either? Just as a left fielder?"

"I didn't say that," Pops answered. "But on the basis of what you've shown me this spring, I know I can't afford to pitch you in a regular turn. I'd have to pick spots for you."

Pops Medlicott was still looking at him in that kindly, school-teacherish way. But Mike knew perfectly well that Pops was telling him, as gently as possible, that this second front-office threat was far more serious, far more final, than the first one had been. Mike remembered vaguely some things he had read about a Washington investigation as to whether baseball was a sport or a business, a monopoly or not a monopoly, and a lot of talk about the inability of players to control their lives. The reserve clause was what they had talked about. He had never understood it and had not paid much attention to it. Now, at this moment, he had an inkling of what it was all about.

If he refused to give up pitching and convert, the front office, using its reserve-clause power, could drop him deeper and deeper into baseball oblivion. At twenty he would be as old and bitter as Slick Hammill was at twenty-six. He no longer saw any way to fight people like Jug Slavin and Stan Davis.

Mike had never known a longer moment in his life than this one, as he stood there facing Pops Medlicott, the kindly, friendly elderly man who peered curiously at him through his rimless glasses, looking as though all he wanted to do was to help Mike Jaffe. Yet Mike knew now—it had gradually dawned on him—that there was pure cold steel behind Pops' seemingly absent-minded words.

Later, Mike had no clear idea of how long he stood in silence, feeling his throat go dry, knowing he was about to make the most important decision of his life so far. He was aware that Pops would say no more; now it was strictly up to Mike himself.

Finally he replied. "I'll play left field today," he said.

"Good boy," Pops said.

CHAPTER

10

MIKE'S recall to the Sox came in June, one day before the major-league trading deadline. They were simply exchanging Blossom for Jaffe, and no one was surprised, least of all Mike.

He was hitting .362 for the Blues now, second best in the league. He was near the top in home runs and runs batted in, despite the fact that he had been in only one game out of four during that first month, his "pitching" month. On the other hand, Blossom's average was an undistinguished .257 for his part-time duty with the Sox, and his extra-base blows had been few and far between. Mike had seen it coming as he checked the progress of the Blue Sox in the sports pages every day. They were in third place now, two games behind the Redskins, five behind the league-leading Clippers.

No one on the Blues tried to conceal his envy when Mike picked up his gear in the clubhouse just before he left. He was not returning as he had come —in an upper berth. He was returning by plane, first class. He could already taste those steaks you ate so often and so casually when you traveled with the Sox.

Slick Hammill didn't hold out his hand when he said good-by. "Luck, kid," he said to Mike. "You sold out. But—luck, anyway."

Mike didn't reply. Inwardly he agreed with Slick; he felt like a man who had sold out. But even though he had done what he'd done in order to save himself from the greased chute leading to Single-A and B and C and maybe D, he remained a pitcher in his own mind. He would bide his time and, meanwhile, bow to the front-office threat that was too much for him now. Later on they would find out they hadn't really licked him; they had just forced him into a strategic retreat, like an army that needs time to regroup its forces before making the big push.

Bob Cosier gave him a handshake, but a limp one. Cosier, who was always looking for an angle for himself, said, "That Madigan must be slowing down on third by now. Any time you feel like mentioning how I play third base and how I hit, well, feel free to do it, Mike." Mike nodded.

Carl Perutz slapped him on the back. "Maybe we'll be playing on the same team next year, who knows?"

"It could be," Mike said, wondering if Perutz wasn't aware that Stretch Stookey still had seven or eight good years ahead of him.

"If not there," Perutz said, with a sardonic shrug of his shoulders, "then maybe here."

"I don't think I'll be back, Carl," Mike said. "Not ever again. One way or another, I'll stick."

"That's what I said three years ago," Perutz said. "And I'll say it again when they call me down to Glensota in the spring."

Pops Medlicott was waiting for him at the clubhouse door when he had finally said good-by to all of them. Mike was carrying two brand-new suitcases he had bought an hour after he had heard the news. Most of the Blue Sox players had expensive-looking luggage, he had noticed, and now he had the same. Pops Medlicott said, "I'll walk outside with you, Mike, while we find you a taxi." Mike nodded as the two headed down the tunnel toward the players' entrance.

"One thing I wanted to say to you, Mike," Pops said. "When you get there, don't carry any chips around on your shoulder, because they insisted you quit pitching. They did it for your own good."

"Or theirs," Mike said.

"Both. No telling how many years you'd have kicked around the bush leagues as a pitcher. But here you are, in one month, headed back up where you belong."

Mike didn't say anything.

"I'm proud of you," Pops said, "for making the decision."

"My father wouldn't be," Mike said.

"I don't believe it," Pops said. "Look, son. I sent them a report on you, naturally. I told them you ought to play around at shortstop a lot for a while during batting practice. Your biggest weakness in the outfield is charging a ground ball. Don't get discouraged if they work you pretty hard on that and a couple of other things."

They were emerging upon the street now. It was a nice day for flying, bright and almost cloudless.

"What other things?"

"Not too much. When you play the position more, you'll start to size up where you should throw the ball—if it comes your way—before the hitter hits it. Right now you don't. I've told you before. You wait until you get your hands on the ball and then make up your mind. You give away an extra base to a runner now and then, because you lose seconds that way. After a while it'll all come naturally, the way driving a car comes naturally after you drive long enough."

A taxi cruised along and Pops hailed it. Mike shoved his luggage inside and turned to shake hands with him. Pops gripped his hand tightly. "I just hope you realize how lucky you are, getting back up there this fast," he said.

"In a way I'm lucky," Mike said. "In a way I'm not."

"Give it everything, Mike. Don't hold back a thing."

"So long, Pops. I liked playing for you."

"So long, son."

On the way to the airport, the driver said, "When you get there, Mike, hit one for me."

Mike felt pleased that he had been instantly recognized. He looked at the name on the identification photo of the driver. "I'll try to, Herman."

"Most of us who were rooting for you are glad you're over that pitching bug, Mike."

"I don't know yet," Mike said, "that I am over it, Herman."

CHAPTER

11

FOR a six-footer only twenty years old, Mike Jaffe was remarkably well filled out in a solid bone-and-muscle way. In fact, from the back, where you could not see the boyishness of his face, he looked every inch a man.

He strode purposefully through the players' gate at the Blue Sox Stadium and the old guy, Maxie, who had been standing guard there since before Mike Jaffe was born, gave him a big welcoming grin. He held out his hand and Mike shook it. "I had a notion you'd be along in time for today's game," Maxie said. "We can sure use that big stick of yours."

Mike wondered if he would be able to get over his quick twinge of resentment when people praised his hitting, of which they had actually seen very

[80]

little, and ignored his pitching, of which they had seen a fair amount. "We'll see, Maxie," Mike told him, as he moved on down the concrete ramp and through the tunnel that led under the stands to the clubhouse.

It was a big, cheerful room with tall windows and wide lockers and a maze of king-sized overhead fans. At the far end were the long rubbing tables, electric diathermy machines, and a whirlpool bath. As Mike walked in, he heard voices pitched in a low key. There was no horseplay going on. There was a worried feel to the atmosphere, and anyone could tell this was not a first-place team. Not at the moment, anyway.

At the big table that served as a desk, near the center, Madigan and Woodward were autographing baseballs. Stretch Stookey, in his underwear, stood with one foot on the bench in front of his locker, reading a letter. Lasky, in front of his, was reading a copy of *The Sporting News*. Nearby, a sports columnist named Ed Daly was interviewing Willie (the Lion) Simms.

"How many ball games," Mike heard Daly ask, "do you figure you've caught, out there in the bull pen, I mean?"

"I don't precisely know," the Lion said, "but I

figure I've caught as many out there as Pete Gibbs has caught behind that plate."

Mike stood very still for a moment before anyone noticed his entrance. Even though the Blue Sox had called him back, were eager to have him with them, he felt a certain reluctance about making this appearance. Every one of them knew he had been trapped by a front-office plot and that, in a sense, he had quit on himself. He sort of felt the way he imagined a rich man's son might feel if he gave up his dreams of becoming an artist or a musician and went to work in his father's bank.

He suddenly remembered his early sand-lot days and the impatience with which he had played the outfield while waiting his turn to do some of the pitching. He had concentrated so fiercely on learning control and a change-up and other things that he had never felt much of a kick in snaring a fly ball. In a way he had always liked to hit, but he had never striven for perfection at the plate. He had always studied hitters with a pitcher's eye, ferreting out little weaknesses that he might exploit when he faced them on the mound. His father had instilled and encouraged this attitude in him, so whatever he happened to know about hitting must be purely accidental, he figured.

Mike had started to cross the room toward Jug Slavin's office when Madigan spied him. "Look who's here!" Madigan shouted. "Big Slug from the Blues!"

In a moment they were all around him, pumping his hand and slapping his back, saying a lot of things that he knew added up to a sincere and joyful welcome home. But again he felt those tiny twinges of resentment, because not a single voice among them expressed the slightest bit of sympathy for his having resigned himself to do what he did not want to do.

Finally he broke away from them. The door to Slavin's office was wide open, so he walked right in. Jug was sitting behind his green, businesslike desk, reading a newspaper. He stood up and thrust his hand across the top of the desk, then waved Mike to a seat beside it.

"The reports on you from Pops Medlicott are even better than I'd hoped," Jug said.

"I was hitting pretty well, I guess," Mike said.

"You'll never regret the decision you made. I'll guarantee you that."

Mike didn't say anything.

"With pitching out of your mind, you can become just about as good a hitter as you want to be."

"You'd have a better idea about that than I

would," Mike said. "But one thing I want to get clear, Mr. Slavin, pitching isn't out of my mind. I can't honestly say that."

"It will be," Jug said. "You just give this team everything you've got, and I mean *everything*, up at the plate and out in the field."

"Nobody fooled me," Mike said. "I knew if I didn't give in they'd keep on dropping me down and down in the minors until I did."

Jug was frowning at him now. "If you go around carrying a grudge against the people who run this club you'll wind up being nothing, neither a hitter nor a pitcher."

He stood up to let Mike know the talk was over. Mike could see he was angry. He said, "Get into uniform. Get up on the field early. Be the first *and* the last to take batting practice. Go out to left field and shag flies when you're not hitting. And just remember: you never made this club as a pitcher and you've got a long way to go to make it as a hitter."

"Is that all?" Mike said.

"For now, yes," Jug said, and turned his back to reach for something behind him.

CHAPTER

12

THE veteran Luke Bates, who had done most of the work out in left field for the Sox so far this year, was a ballplayer of the old school, right down to the pouch of chewing tobacco in his cheek. He slammed into a pivot man without mercy, breaking up a double play. He crashed walls in pursuit of long fly balls. He ran out hopeless infield pop-ups with all the drive and hustle of a man who has laid down a neat bunt along the third-base line. Now crowding forty, he still played the game with all the dedication he had shown as a teen-age busher. Healthy, or hobbled by injuries, he didn't know how to give anything less than his best to a team.

The sports writers knew it and showed their deep respect for him in what they wrote. Enemy ballplayers knew it and showed theirs by taking no chances, even at his advanced age, with his arm or his pistonlike drive on the base paths. And of course his teammates knew it, so they listened to what he had to say and treated him as though he were still in his famous prime.

Everyone knew he was living on borrowed big-league time now. When the Sox had pulled him back from the Association, they gave him a crack at his fifteenth big-league season, and he had had a half dozen minor-league years to begin with.

"Some credit," Jug Slavin had said to a reporter on the bench before Mike's first game, "for the fighting atmosphere of the team, in spite of our slow start, must go to Bates. From the day he arrived here, when we signed him as a free agent to help fill a serious gap, he's been a battler. He never quits. He never thinks a game is lost. He works like a hungry rookie and his attitude sets an example for the rest of the team. They have to strain to keep up with him. He'll beat your brains out, but he's positively a spiritual leader, besides."

Mike knew all this about Luke Bates. He had been around long enough now so that he wasn't awed by big names in the baseball world very often, but Luke Bates awed him. As Mike stood in the batter's box during batting practice, he knew that Bates was leaning on one of the pipes of the cage behind him, watching. He had a desire to impress Bates. It was funny in a way. They were both after the same job, out in left field, but Mike had no sense of jealousy or competition where Bates was concerned. He didn't know why that was, unless it was because Bates was near the end of his string and he was at the beginning of his.

Anyway, he swung hard and pulled the first lob delivered to him. He had read in the sports pages how writers described him at the plate, as "sinewy," "graceful," "packed with power," and full of "wrist action." He thought, when he connected with the first lob, that he backed up all those compliments. He knew he'd broken his wrists at the exact last split second, like a good golfer. He knew the power of his big shoulders was all behind the swing. He knew he had come around on the ball with an easy grace. And the flight of the ball proved to him that he was right. It ripped its way through an unfriendly wind blowing in stiffly from the left-field wall. It had wings. Not for a moment did the wind make it falter. It rose and rose and disappeared out of sight, headed for the railroad tracks beyond the confines of the ball park.

Mike heard the contented *ah* that came from the early-bird fans scattered in the seats. "Boom!" somebody yelled from behind. "Get the tape measure!" "Do it again, Mike!"

He planted his feet widely and brought the clenched bat back so that it was parallel with his right shoulder. He crouched just a little bit. His jaw was outthrust, giving him the look of a hitter who is daring a pitcher to knock him down. He wasn't thinking of the fans who had yelled happily at his first wallop, or of Jug Slavin watching from the step of the dugout; he was thinking of Luke Bates. He wanted Bates's admiration. In his eagerness he swung at a ball that was too high, too much outside. The result was an easy loft back of the second-base bag.

Then he rapped one line drive after another, holding back from the bad pitches, clipping the good ones. Three times his line drives made an echoing whack against the left-field wall, and twice they cleared it. When he stepped out of the box to let Madigan take his turn, Madigan said out of the side of his mouth, "I'll bet you can't bunt, Bruiser."

"I *forgot* to bunt!" Mike said.

"Never mind. You won't have to," Madigan said.

Mike headed for the dugout to get his glove before going out to left field to shag flies. He knew already that Jug Slavin did not plan to use him today, or else Jug would not wear him out this way before game time. Someone tapped him on the back, and even before he turned around he had a feeling it was Luke Bates. He had wanted to approach Bates, but he knew it was proper for the older ballplayer to make the advances to the younger one.

"Mike," Luke Bates said, "I want to talk to you."

"Sure," Mike said.

"They just told me you and I are going to be roommates for a while—for as long as we're on speaking terms, that is."

"No kidding," Mike said. "That's great with me."

"Me too. Listen, I watched you bat. You're a hitter."

"I never hit too much," Mike said. "I always pitched. My father always wanted me to be a pitcher, and that's what I wanted to be."

Luke nodded. "I know. Your old man had a real good curve ball. He might have made it except for that arm trouble. . . ."

"You mean you knew my father?"

"I played two years with him. When we were with the Albany Senators seventeen, eighteen years ago.

You were still in a play pen then, but he already knew you'd wind up in the big leagues."

"As a pitcher," Mike said.

Bates shrugged. "The main thing is, you wound up in the big leagues. He'd be happy about that. Plenty happy."

"I don't know," Mike said.

"Well, I do."

Mike wanted to keep talking with Luke Bates, but he heard Jug Slavin's voice behind him. "All right, Mike. Let's see you go after some of those fly balls out there. On the double."

Mike nodded back at Luke Bates as he headed toward the dugout for his glove. But he didn't do it on the double. He strolled in, then strolled out toward the field. He wanted to talk to Luke Bates about his father right then a lot more than he wanted to chase a bunch of foolish fly balls in left field.

CHAPTER

13

MIKE watched the ball game from the dugout, sitting beside Jug Slavin, because Jug had arranged it that way. There were a lot of things Jug wanted to point out to him as the game progressed. Mostly they concerned fielding and hitting. Mike kept nodding, but all the time his eyes and his mind strayed to the pitcher's mound. He kept watching Joe Rodriguez, who was pitching for the Sox, and Tom Count, the fine left-hander of the Redskins. It was a pitcher's game.

In the second inning, with no score, the Redskins put a man on third with two outs. Voccola, the Redskins' right fielder, hit a long, sleepy fly ball to deep left. It was one of those balls that lack real force, and it looked as if it would come down and slap the left-field wall for a long single or a double. Voccola was fast and the chances were it would be a double. But in either case, the first run of the ball game would cross the plate.

Luke Bates had started back when the ball caromed from Voccola's bat in high flight. There seemed to be no room at all for a catch. But Bates tore back as though no left-field wall existed. He leaped high, his back seemingly pressed flat against the wall, and he came down with the ball riveted in the pocket of his glove. That ended the threat.

"See," Jug said, leaning toward Mike. "That Luke. . . . He goes for the wall as naturally as wood burns."

Mike nodded, but he was wondering what Rodriguez had thrown Voccola and why Voccola had been able to get that much height and distance on the ball. The way he figured it, and he was watching each pitch the way a pickerel watches a traveling minnow, Rodriguez had meant to keep the ball lower; but his control had been just slightly off.

"I see," Mike said to Jug.

In the fourth inning, the score still nothing to nothing, Madigan stepped in after Tom Count had retired the entire Sox line-up without a man's reaching first. Madigan accepted two strikes and then, with a nothing-and-two count against him, he withstood a batter's natural temptation, fear, and nervousness in such a situation, and ran the count to three and two.

"You can't appreciate Madigan fully," Jug said to Mike, "until you've seen him operate for years. How many clubs have a genuine lead-off man, put him there, and keep him there? Most ballplayers who bat lead-off eventually run into trouble. In that spot you have to take a lot of pitches; it's your job. That can lead to slumps, because it's your duty to let so many good ones go by. Madigan forces more work out of a pitcher than any other man in the league, so what if he does bat only .260?"

The three-and-two pitch came in and Madigan became a small sprung trap. Outfielders didn't play him deep, because he was a puncher, not a driver; but he really gave this one a ripple. The ball cleared the upstretched glove of the leaping Redskin short-stop and found its jetlike way into a small pocket between the left and center fielders. When it was retrieved, Madigan was on third base, and any dreams of a perfect game that Tom Count might have cherished had gone up the chimney. It looked now as if it would be easy for the Sox to break the scoreless deadlock. The top of the order was coming up and no one was out. But Tom Count was no ordinary pitcher.

The infield crept in on Chip Fiske, who could lay down a bunt like a billiard shot. He didn't, though. Instead, he hit the second pitch, trying to pull it toward first and get the run in. It might even go through for a single as well.

Fiske bargained without success. The ball he got his bat on, Mike saw in his concentration on the pitcher, was a curve that went inside and down. Mike wasn't at all surprised at what happened, and instead of feeling downcast at the result, he could not help but feel a glow of admiration for the way Tom Count had handled Fiske. The ball behaved as it had to, since it was pitched to just the right spot: it bounced back easily to Tom Count, who turned threateningly to Madigan, who, in turn, moved back toward the bag. Then Count tossed Fiske out at first, and Madigan remained on third with one out and two to go.

Up stepped the switch hitter, Russ Woodward. Russ batted right-handed against Tom Count. He went to two balls and one strike and then he laced one. It was a screamer. It shot toward the edge of the left foul line, but well inside. Instinctively Madigan had started for home; just as instinctively the

Redskin third baseman, Al Skiff, went into the air, Roman-candle style. He came down with the ball and jumped for the bag. Madigan had become aware of the danger, but it didn't look as though he had done so in time.

Madigan didn't slide back; he dove. Skiff was diving too, and the picture they presented made Mike think of two dogs fighting over an old bone. Madigan, the pros' pro, won the bone.

Two outs now, but the runner was still on third.

Now the Blue Sox problem of the season presented itself. As in so many games, the big job was dropped into the lap of the clean-up hitter. Almost every three days, as Mike well knew from reading the papers, the Sox used a new clean-up man. Today the task had been awarded to Pete Gibbs. Luke Bates was batting sixth, because base hits had not been rattling off his bat of late.

The big, rangy catcher was still a picture-book hitter, even though he didn't rate the clean-up spot in a batting order. His average wasn't that strong. He was a solid fifth- or sixth-place batter, and occasionally he had a hitting streak; but he was not an authentic clean-up man.

Jug was talking into Mike's ear again. "When Pete's timing is right," he said, "nobody looks better up there. But when it's wrong, nobody looks worse."

Mike nodded. He was wondering what Tom Count would feed Gibbs. He was thinking what he himself would throw in Tom Count's spot, now that the big jam was almost unjammed. Almost, except for Gibbs.

He was inside Tom Count's mind now. Would I walk him and set up the force at second? Andy Pearson followed today, then Luke Bates, and Stretch Stookey next, dropped down to seventh because of the southpaw pitching. Actually, Mike thought to himself, this is a spot where nine out of ten clean-up batters would get the intentional walk. But Pearson was a clutch hitter, even though he was no slugger. Therefore, Mike decided, personally he would pitch to Gibbs. And as he made up his mind, the weakness of the Sox clean-up spot became deadly apparent.

Evidently Tom Count figured the same way. He was still pitching from a stretch position as he had since Madigan had weighed in at third. He threw a very sharp curve ball that caught the inside corner for strike one. He threw the very same ball again, which didn't surprise Gibbs, but it was just too tough a ball to get a piece of. This was beautiful control, especially for a left-hander.

Mike's thoughts about the third pitch concerned Tom Count, not Pete Gibbs. He could not help but admire the superb job Count was doing to hold back the run that Madigan represented. The waste pitch is due, Mike thought. But I wouldn't throw it, not now. Gibbs is bothered.

Mike knew in the next instant that he was figuring exactly the way Count was figuring. The ball came straight down the middle, really eye-blinking in its ferocious speed, and Gibbs reacted too late. He got a miserable little piece of it, and it went up into the air midway between the plate and first base. Hertz, the Redskin first baseman, swooped it into his fishnet type glove, and that was that.

It had been breath-taking to Mike. Breathtaking, though, in terms of Tom Count's skill. That kind of job, he knew so well, was something a pitcher thought about for weeks, just before he fell asleep. There was no thrill like it, never could be. The home-run thrill—that was for people who had never known the big one. He and Tom Count knew the big one.

CHAPTER
14

THERE was absolutely nothing Mike could do about it. He could only get really absorbed in what the pitchers were doing. Fine fielding plays, clean line drives, long balls that found the empty spots in the vastness of the outfield—these things made the crowd roar. They pained Mike; they merely meant that an error of omission or commission had been committed by the pitcher. His sympathy was always with the pitcher, even when the Sox were at bat.

There was one exception to this feeling, and that, of course, came when he faced a pitcher himself. That didn't happen often during the remainder of this home stand—just twice, in fact.

Jug kept him glued to his side on the bench every day. Jug made him take twice and sometimes three times the number of batting-practice cuts of any other man on the team. Jug made him run his legs off in left field, chasing flies before game time. Fiske and Woodward and Luke Bates, especially, commented on what he did right and what he did wrong. He was not unappreciative of this prince-like treatment, but it just didn't mean as much to him as the times when Lasky would sit on the bench beside him—when he could break away from Jug Slavin and all Jug's talk about fielding and hitting. Anyway, Mike and Eddie Lasky would study the pitchers, and these were the sessions Mike really liked.

"That guy," Lasky said one day, "going out there for the Panthers today—he looks easy. He isn't. Have you noticed? We're hitting his first pitch most of the time. That's Marv Newman. Maybe you don't especially know his name."

"I've heard it," Mike said. "But I don't know that he did anything that I can remember."

"Well, you'll remember him gradually," Lasky said. "Newman is giving them what I'd call a three-quarter-speed pitch. It's got a little fade to it. This is no secret. I already told Jug."

"What's good about it?" Mike asked, as anxious to find out as a hunter who's just been told there are pheasants around.

"What's good about it," Lasky explained, "is this. It's the kind of harmless-looking pitch that makes everybody say, 'This guy hasn't got it today.' And it looks as if he hadn't."

"But he has?"

"He has. You'll see. I told Jug. We'll keep popping up on this guy Newman. We'll pop and pop."

"You ought to be a manager," Mike said.

"I will be," Lasky said. "Don't worry your young head about that."

Mike liked to sit with Lasky even better than he liked to sit with Jug Slavin. Lasky had the makings of a manager, he was sure of that. In addition, Lasky always knew what pitchers were up to. He also knew batters, in many ways.

The Sox were behind, 0 to 3. They had been popping up, as Lasky had predicted. Walker popped up twice in a row, in almost exactly the same spot, to the third baseman. When he came back into the dugout, Lasky looked at him in a friendly sort of sour way, and said, "Bud, boy, you're just knockin' that old sky black and blue. You gotta stop it."

Instead of getting irritated, Walker said, "What am I doing wrong?"

"You think it's coming in fast and it comes in three-quarters, is all," Lasky said.

Walker sat down and watched Newman make his delivery.

Things went on like this. Mike could not get half as interested in what Jug Slavin had to say about fielders and hitters as in what Lasky said about pitchers and what they were doing. He thought that if he owned a ball club, Lasky would be his manager, not Jug Slavin.

Mike went to bat first in a game against the Panthers. It was the last half of the eighth, and the Sox were behind, 4 to 6. Luke Bates was on third as the result of a walk, and a single by Stookey. Mike hit for Phil Doyle, who had relieved Bix Hanson, who had showed he didn't especially have it that day. The crowds let out a whoop, rather than a roar, when he walked up to the plate. He didn't feel any pressure on himself. He never did. He still thought the way a pitcher thinks: any hit you get is gravy—no big things expected.

No matter. When Mike set his sights, he wanted to hit. He took one on the edge of the plate that he knew would be a strike, but the pitch was not for him. He never worried about having one or even two strikes called on him. He could always see the ball, looming up big, and he knew he could almost always get a piece of it, no matter what. A second pitch came in, and it was really wide. The third one was wide too. So it was two and one, and he felt the big one coming.

He was right. It came in. It was a slightly uncertain curve ball, and it hung a little. He came around on it and felt the power behind his smash, but he didn't look as he raced down the path. He had a feeling the ball was on its way toward deep left center, but he also had a feeling it would not make the seats.

It didn't. There were two outs, so it had to reach the wall or it would be nothing—just a long out. He looked up as he rounded first, and he saw that the Panther center fielder was getting close. He kept churning and, to his amazement, the ball didn't dip; it kept on its high line. The Panther center fielder leaped high, but he couldn't do anything. The ball had such fierce power that it hit high on the wall and cracked off to the right. Mike knew by now that he had a triple.

A triple it was, and it tied the score. A moment later Madigan chopped a sickly little grounder that found its way between first and second, and the Sox were in front, 7 to 6.

That was the final score. Bernie Glaser came in and finished the ninth, and not a Panther reached first. Back in the clubhouse, Mike was still amazed that the ball he had hit had not been caught. It had not lost altitude as most balls do.

"That one," Madigan said to him in the shower, "you really clobbered."

"It didn't feel so good," Mike said.

"It looked good," Madigan said.

"I had a feeling the guy sort of fooled me," Mike insisted.

"He fooled you the way a fly fools a spider," Madigan told him.

It felt good to get a hit, of course, but Mike still felt that when he got one it was really an accident. This feeling never left him.

The second time he got a chance to hit during this home stand, the Sox were again in a serious predicament, although they had runners on every base. This time they were not behind; the score was tied. Mike hit for Harry Diefendorf, who had held the Bears to one run in nine full innings. The trouble was, the Sox had also managed to get only one run in all that time.

Mike swung hard on the first pitch and missed a sharp curve. He watched the second one go by, because it looked bad to him, but the umpire called it a second strike. He didn't protest, but Jug came running out of the dugout to yell about it. Then, because there were two outs and two strikes against him, he went for a bad pitch. It was high and outside, and as soon as he brought the bat around he knew he should never have offered. He just managed to get a faint piece of it, and he started to run.

The burst of noise from the crowd, strangely enough, sounded cheerful. This, he was sure, was a sad pop fly. In a way, it was. It hoisted itself along the right-field foul line, the opposite field for him. It kept on hoisting itself, though it was soft and by no means power-laden. But somehow it came down to rest just inside the right-field foul pole, where a man in a red hunting cap caught it in the second row.

It was the cheapest home run Mike had ever hit, and he had hit it on the nothing-and-two count, and it had not felt good. On the other hand, it was the first grand slam he had to his credit so far in either the majors or the minors.

Later, in the dressing room, Fiske said, "I thought you bunted, but I wasn't sure."

"I never hit a ball worse," Mike said.

"It was miserable," Gibbs said. "I'll put it that way."

CHAPTER
15

ONCE more Mike was off on a Western trip. He had taken them for two full years, but it had been different then. At the outset he had always known that there was little chance of his seeing action. Usually he would sit on the bench or warm up in the bull pen, but unless a game was one-sided, he would never be called in. Now it was different. Now, he knew, he could very well be in the starting line-up of any game at all, and he might be in there to stay.

Even though Luke Bates had tailed off somewhat from his early-spring outburst, he was still hitting what the broadcasters liked to call a "solid .290." Luke was having trouble with his legs, however—something described as shin splints. In their room at night on the train going West (the Sox only flew when they had to and most of them did not like the idea at all), Luke kept hammering things into Mike's head. "You've got the greatest opportunity a kid ever had," he said. "Why, there's no telling what you might do. I can't define it—nobody can—but when you take a cut at a ball it's a sort of natural perfection."

"Did you ever see me pitch?" Mike asked.

"No, and I don't especially want to," Luke said.

"Why not?"

"Because I've looked at you up at that plate, and I know hitting is what you were meant to do."

"My father didn't think so."

"Your father would have changed his mind, believe me. Sure, he was a pitcher—a good one, too, and if he hadn't had that arm trouble he would have made it. But he was meant to be a pitcher. That's all he was looking at when he looked at you—the pitching. If your father could see you today, he'd say just what I'm saying."

"Maybe," Mike said. "I'm not so sure about that."

The Blue Sox' first Western stop was the home park of the Hawks, a fine park for hitters. The fences were not too far away and they did not have commercial advertising; they were painted a solid green. This background gave the man at the plate good vision. And the wind frequently blew toward the outfield.

Mike had a feeling he was going to start the game, not just because Luke Bates was bothered by shin splints, but chiefly because Jug Slavin had told him not to shag flies in batting practice.

Shortly before the game began, Jug waved him over. "You're in today, Mike," he said. "I'm batting you clean-up."

Mike nodded. He supposed some rookies would have jumped for joy if the manager had come over and told them this. He felt good about it, but he did not feel like jumping for joy. He went over to the bench and started to talk to Phil Doyle, the number one relief man. "Were you always a reliever, Phil?" he asked.

"Ever since Wichita," Phil said. "That was quite a few years ago. I think I had just passed my Eagle Scout test."

Mike knew he was joking. "You like relieving better than starting?"

"It's a living," Phil said.

"You worked up a big reputation in a hurry, relieving," Mike said to him.

Phil rested his elbows on his knees and his chin

on his hands. He stared out at the field. "You can have all the glory and the gold of the bull pen. I'd like to be a starter."

"I know what you mean," Mike said. "So would I."

He was still thinking of that conversation when he came to bat in the first inning. Fiske was on first. Madigan had flied out and Woodward had howled violently at a third called strike. The Hawks had their only first-class pitcher going for them today, Peach McNamara, a long, dark left-hander with a fuzzy look and a fuzzy fast ball. He seemed to deliver it in slow motion with a drawn-out, easy stretch.

Peach stretched and the ball came in. He caught the inside corner, and Mike knew he had been thoroughly fooled. The next ball, deceptively fast after that slow motion, caught the outside corner, and Mike went for it. He practically had to. He knew, as he did so, that his timing had been knocked out by this strategy. Because he got only a tiny piece of the ball he just popped it into the stands, to his right and behind him. Now he was in the hole.

McNamara wasted two balls on him. The big one came in, and this time Mike knew it was faster than it looked. He nailed it. He knew the ball was really rammed. He had the feeling that a baseball couldn't be hit much harder than he'd hit that one. It was low, just above the grass blades, and it drove past the Hawks' lunging third baseman, sprayed chalk dust on the left-field line, and shot into the deepest corner of left field, on the ground.

Mike saw, as he rounded first, that the left fielder was not playing the carom too well. He saw Fiske was about to reach third, with no sign of stopping. Mike reached second, slowed down, and stopped. He realized, after he had stopped, that Fido Murphy, in the third-base coaching box, had been wigwagging him on. But it was too late. Anyway, he was on second and the run was in.

Gibbs, batting fifth today, spun a grounder to second which looked like an easy out. But the Hawks' second baseman fussed around with it long enough for Gibbs to reach first while Mike moved on to third. It came to him then that if he had made his double the triple that it should have been, he would have carried the second Sox run across on this bobble.

Pearson struck out and that ended the inning.

When Mike went in to get his glove from the dugout, Jug Slavin was waiting for him. "Take a shower," Jug said.

"For what?" Mike demanded.

"For you know what," Jug said.

Luke Bates was already trotting out to left field, and Mike went into the tunnel alongside the dugout and headed toward the showers.

CHAPTER

16

JUG SLAVIN never spoke of this incident to Mike during the remainder of the Hawk series. Nor did Jug take him off the bench. Luke Bates spoke of it, though; he brought it up that night, in their hotel room. "There was no reason for you to stop at second," Luke said. "You were being flagged on from third, and you had plenty of time to see that you'd hit the ball so hard the left fielder couldn't handle the rebound. Why did you park, like a taxi, at second?"

"I don't like to slide if I don't have to," Mike said. "I've seen good pitchers hurt their arms that way."

"Listen," Luke said. "You're no more a pitcher than I am. And I wish I could be half, just a measly half, the hitter you are."

Mike was silent.

"You go all out when you make a hit, or you won't go anywhere in the big leagues, except back to the showers again."

"I drove in the run," Mike said.

"And wasted the second one. It turned out we didn't need it, but it doesn't usually turn out that way. You sitting on second there. . . . I've seen pennants lost by that little. Baseball is a game of inches. You've heard that, haven't you?"

"No," Mike said.

"Well, it is, and it's a crime for guys like you, who can hit that ball, not to do everything to make the most of it. Watch the .240 hitters and you'll learn something. When they slug a ball, which isn't often, they make the most of it. But you lucky guys. . . ."

Luke turned out the light and they went to sleep.

The Sox took two out of three from the Hawks, which was no great feat, since the Hawks were generally regarded as the door mats of the league. They moved on to the park of the Panthers. A left-hander, Milt Greene, was scheduled to pitch for the home club, against Bix Hanson. Mike remembered he had once hit—pinch-hit—a home run against Greene to break up a ball game his second year on the Sox bench. He wasn't too surprised when Jug Slavin told him that he was playing.

"We'll forget about that bush business of yours with the Hawks," Jug said. "Any time you show me you mean business, you're in this line-up to stay. Is that clear?"

Mike nodded.

"Does the idea interest you?" Jug asked sarcastically.

Mike nodded again.

"Your enthusiasm overwhelms me," Jug said.

Mike went over to the water cooler and talked awhile with George Wettling, the Sox batting-practice pitcher. George had known good days in this league, many seasons of them. He had always been a spot control man, which was why he now was such a good batting-practice pitcher.

"When you gonna get in that line-up again?" George asked.

"I'm supposed to play today," Mike said.

"*Supposed to!*" George said. "Are you against the idea?"

"I'm for it," Mike said. "You threw me a lot of bad balls in batting practice."

"That happens some days, even to us batting-practice pitchers," George said. "You take me. They called me a good control pitcher, and I must have been. My bases-on-balls record was right up there."

"I thought, lobbing them in that way, you could put a ball just about where a batter wanted it."

"Not so," George said. "Even in batting practice you sometimes try and try to get a ball to a particular spot, and you can't. That was how it was with me today. I didn't have it."

It was just one more of the mysteries of pitching that never failed to fascinate Mike. Everything about the art of pitching still gripped him the way it had since his sand-lot days. But—

There was a good weekday crowd. The Blue Sox always drew well, all around the league. The Panthers were only two games behind them, and that added a lot to the interest of this game. When it started, the park was at least half full, and a lot of the fans in left field yelled at Mike during fielding practice.

"You're all mixed up, kid! The bull pen is in *right* field!"

"Here comes a fly. Watch out for your head!"

"You've got that glove on the wrong hand!"

It was good-natured kidding, and Mike didn't mind it. At least, they knew he was really a pitcher, not a left fielder.

It turned out to be the kind of ball game that Mike liked; time and again it hung on just one pitch.

Going into the top of the seventh, Bix Hanson had given the Panthers four hits and no runs; Milt Greene had given the Sox no runs and no hits. The buzz in the stands, over a possible no-hitter, had already started when Mike led off the inning.

Mike had previously laced a hard ball down the third-base line but had been thrown out by a step. Then he had flied deep to center. Now, as he stepped in, he remembered that pinch-hit homer he had tagged Greene for, two years ago. Most hitters, he knew, never forgot such a thing. It had seemed less important to him, but he had a notion he had hit a curve ball that hadn't been too sharp, and that had come right after a let-up. Not that this necessarily meant anything, but he knew that hitters tried to remember these things.

Greene finished his warm-up tosses. He was rated as a pitcher with a lot of know-how, and he had one of the best sliders around. Last year he had pitched the only no-hitter in the league, against the dismal Hawks. Now he looked down to Hawes, his catcher, for the sign. A new ball had been given to him, and he tried rubbing a wrinkle into it. Then he stepped on the rubber and went into his motion.

The ball came in fast, rather high, and Mike picked on it. It went where so many of his balls went—hard toward left, but on the ground. Broome, the Panther third baseman, backhanded it and straightened to throw to first but stopped as it was called foul.

The second pitch was a fast ball too, down around the knees. Mike let it go by. It was a ball, but close.

Hawes wheeled angrily to protest. "Down the pipe!" he snarled. "Right down there."

The umpire said nothing.

"You saw it!" Hawes snapped. "You *must* have. You've got a good seat here to see what's going on."

"Two minutes," the umpire said. "You've got two minutes left."

Hawes squatted down behind the plate, his scowl showing through his mask. "You," he muttered to Mike. "You built any good model airplanes lately?"

"Is that supposed to be a joke?" Mike asked him.

"One minute," the umpire said.

Hawes gave Greene the sign, and Greene wound up. The hush in the stands emphasized the importance of every pitch now. Greene was still nine outs away from a perfect game, but the way his curves were breaking and his fast ball crackling made anything look possible today.

From the Sox bench Mike heard some Spanish

words coming forth. That would be Joe Rodriguez, who was a very successful bench jockey; he could say whatever he wanted to, for usually no one could understand him. But it was different today. The Panthers had a Venezuelan utility infielder named Tico Colavo, and it was he who answered Rodriguez. In a moment a violent exchange of Spanish utterances sprang up, and both Hawes and the umpire were as bewildered as anyone else about what was going on. All they could tell was that noise was being produced. Who was insulting whom was a secret to everyone except Rodriguez and Colavo.

The remarks subsided, and Greene pitched. The pitch was high and inside, and Mike took it, running the count to two and one. Then a strike was poured over the outside corner and it was all even between Greene and Jaffe.

Mike was sure that if he broke up this no-hitter of Greene's with a long drive, an announcer up in the broadcasting booth would be sure to say, "Well, Jaffe laid the lumber to that one," or, "Well, Jaffe met that one right where the signature is." He knew just what must be going on in Greene's mind, knew what a thrill it would be to him if he lasted through the seventh, with a second no-hitter still going for him. That ominous hush from the crowd grew even louder in its complete silence. And then the pitch came in, low and outside, and if Greene and Hawes thought they were dealing with an overanxious rookie, they saw they were wrong. He let it go by. The count was three and two now. Even the benches became completely silent. An airplane, droning overhead, produced the only murmur of sound at this moment.

Mike saw that the outfield was pulled over toward left all the way. He saw that the infield was deep, the first baseman far off the bag, the second baseman close to his bag, the shortstop deep in the hole, and the third baseman almost standing on the foul line. This all added up to a compliment to him. They were afraid of him, and he knew that batters had not been afraid of him this way when he was on the mound.

There had always been a lot of jokes about left-handers. Goofy guys, they were called. But this Milt Greene was not goofy; he was dead serious. He proved it now by daring to throw a curve ball on the three-and-two pitch—at a tense moment like this, too. It broke as sharply as a pane of glass hit by a rock. It broke right off Mike's fists, but he had to swing; there was nothing else to do at that last split moment when it broke. He hit it where it wound up—right off the fists. The bat split, and the meat end went flying down toward first. He flew after it, and the ball flew—an arching, lazy Texas leaguer—into left field.

The third baseman, the left fielder, and the short-stop went after it with the desperate urgency of a stricken man going after a doctor. The ball not only eluded all three, it took one of those crazy, un-predictable hops and twisted its way toward the foul line.

Tweet Tillman, coaching at first, waved Mike on, and he sped toward second. He saw the play was going to be close, terribly close. He hit the dirt at almost the same instant he saw the ball reaching the second baseman's glove. He slid in; he also slid past the bag. But his reaction was instantaneous. He turned and slapped his left hand onto the bag, staying on the ground for a long moment and get-ting his breath. As he started to get up he heard the groan from the crowd. It rose and didn't die down. He knew how sick the fans and Milt Greene must feel. A no-hitter had been spoiled by a broken-bat pop fly to left. It was the worst thing that could have happened to a conscientious pitcher like Greene.

As Mike prepared to get up, he started to switch

his touch on the bag from his left to his right hand, to make things easier for himself. The instant he started to make the switch, he felt the ball being pounded into his back, saw the umpire shift his palms-flat *safe* signal to his thumb-in-the-air jerk— *out*. Out he was. But at the same time, out the window had flown Milt Greene's superb no-hitter.

When Mike came back to the bench, Jug slapped him on the back. "That could have happened to anybody. I'm sure you won't do it again. You went in there hard, like a ballplayer. You hustled, Mike. All the way."

He should have felt great, but he didn't. When the game ended, the Panthers had won it 2-0, and the only hit made against Milt Greene had been that silly pop-fly thing of Mike Jaffe's. All he could think of was that the single he had hit had done no good. It had only ruined what should have been the second no-hitter of Milt Greene's career. It was a shame.

He felt like a heel.

ED DALY welcomed the team home with a long piece in his morning column the day they returned.

The Blue Sox are home again and they have moved up from third place to second place. This means they made progress in the West, where they had a trip record of eight won and four lost. But before anybody gets starry-eyed about another pennant this year, there are a couple of things we must think about. One of these things is a fellow named Mike Jaffe, the retreaded pitcher, new left fielder, twenty-year-old bonus boy.

Let's start from there.

Without an authentic clean-up man, somebody to back up Russ Woodward, we're nowhere. Let's face that one. In Luke Bates we have a left fielder who will gladly give his right arm any day to help win a ball game. We know that. In Mike Jaffe we have a young player with so much power he could make a bulldozer cringe, but the boy still thinks he's a pitcher. He showed that time after time on the Western trip. His sympathies, even when he's batting, are always with the pitcher. How mixed up can you get?

Here is a hitter who could reach Cooperstown in due time. But he won't, not the way he's going at things. In the few games he has played he is hitting .368 and has slugged most of his hits for extra bases, including three home runs. Kennie Willard, who is so badly missed, never had the potential of Mike Jaffe. But Willard was money in the bank, and Jaffe is money in a bookie's hands, at least right now.

Luke Bates is great. Let's say no more. But when a club keeps shifting its batting order, using a different man in the clean-up spot every second day, it doesn't have a team; it has a mob. You can run a farm system on a big scale, as the Blue Sox do and have done for years, and you still won't come up with a hitter of Jaffe's natural power more than once in ten years. But what good is talent if it isn't used for all it's worth?

Jaffe hits a ball with an easy majesty, but at the same time anyone can see he doesn't really care. He can go after a fly ball well enough to get by, and more than makes up for his fielding with that bat. But since the eight other men playing alongside of him can see that he doesn't really care too much, what does Jaffe do to them? Troublesome players have come up to the Sox before now, and there will probably be more. But if the talents that Mike Jaffe has demonstrated are not backed up by that old will to win, he'll be back with the Blues come July, and the Blue Sox will be back in third place before then.

Mike read the column, Jug Slavin must have read it, and Stan Davis surely did. The upshot—not caused by the column, as Jug carefully pointed out —was a conference among the three of them just before the first game of the home stand, in Jug's office.

"I understand," Stan Davis said, prowling around the room as he talked, "that after you ruined that no-hitter Milt Greene had going, you were expressing sympathy for Greene in the locker room. I have this information from what I consider to be fairly reliable sources."

"I felt sort of bad about it, yes," Mike said.

"*Why?*"

Mike stared at him in amazement. "How could I *not* feel bad? The hit didn't do any good. It ruined things for him, things he'd worked a long time on. It was a lucky, cheap hit. What's wrong about that?"

Davis shoved his cigarette into an ash tray on Jug Slavin's desk and raised his bushy eyebrows. He said to Jug Slavin, "Make it quick. Send him to Keokuk and be done with it."

Jug cleared his throat. "Mike," he said, "I understand how you feel. You haven't really converted yet. We, the whole team, were mighty proud that you prevented Greene from throwing a no-hitter at us that day."

"Well . . ." Mike said.

Stan Davis lumbered over and stood face to face with Mike, as if one large dog were facing another dog down. "Look, son," Davis said. "One thing you must get through that young skull of yours— if you're going to win ball games you can't ever feel any sympathy for the other team. Is that the way you feel?"

Mike thought a moment. "No," he said.

Stan Davis turned to Jug Slavin. "Keokuk," he said. "Fast."

"The thing is, Mike," Jug said quickly, "you're looking out the wrong end of the telescope. Look at it our way. We don't worry about anything at all except beating the other fellow. It's a simple rule of major-league baseball. If that pitcher out there happens to be your brother, you still go after him."

"You won't get it across," Stan Davis said, walking to a far corner of the room and acting as though he wanted to hide. "This lad is the sympathetic type. He's just another one of those nice guys."

"Shut up," Jug said to Stan Davis, and Mike was aware that Jug was taking his life in his hands when he spoke that way to Davis. He looked earnestly at Mike. "Mike, when you face a pitcher, don't you hate him?"

As always, Mike thought the question over. "Not especially," he said.

"So long," Stan Davis said, and stalked out of the room.

"Mike, believe me, boy," Jug said, "you could wind up making maybe sixty thousand dollars a year if you could learn to hate pitchers."

"I can't help but admire them, Mr. Slavin," Mike said. "I might as well give it to you straight. I know what they go through."

"But do you think they think about what *you* go through when you face them?"

"I'll do the best I can," Mike said. "I can promise you that."

Jug Slavin stood up. His face looked a little bit red. "You heard what Mr. Davis said about Keokuk?"

"Where is that, anyway?" Mike asked.

"Pretty soon," Jug Slavin said, "you'll find out."

AFTER that session Mike was sure he would sit on the bench for a while. He was wrong; he was in left field that afternoon again, batting fourth. There was certainly something odd about Jug Slavin and Stan Davis. Why did they bawl him out that way and then not punish him? He was doubly surprised, because this game opened a series with the Clippers, who were in first place by four games. The Clippers, year in and year out, were the biggest threat the Sox faced.

The game turned out to be a picnic for the hitters. No pitcher on either side seemed to have a thing in the parade that followed. The Clippers scored two in the first; the Sox came back with three. Mike drove in one of the runs with a double. The Clippers got two more in the second; the Sox tied the game up with one more and then went ahead with three in the fourth. In this inning Mike belted a ball as hard as any he could remember, but it went to dead center and was caught at the base of the flag-pole out there by Mansell, the Clipper center fielder. However, it did bring in a run from third.

The game continued to seesaw its way through inning after inning and the crowd loved it, even if the pitchers, a total of eight for the two teams, didn't. To Mike the whole thing was a mess. The game was not big-league in any sense. In the bot-tom of the eighth the Sox led, 12 to 10.

At this point Mike came up, with men on first and second, and two outs. Fritz Wesson was going through the motions as the fifth Clipper pitcher. Fritz had an ugly look; he always had needed a shave whenever Mike had seen him, and everyone knew he had a reputation as a dust-off pitcher. He studied Mike with deliberation before he threw the first ball. So far Mike had a double, a long home run to left, the long sacrifice fly to center, a line-drive single to left, and a walk. The Clippers were still in the ball game, for a margin of two runs didn't mean much in this kind of game.

The first pitch that Fritz threw was high, hard,

and inside. From the moment it left his hand, Mike was sure Fritz had aimed it at his head. You could never prove these things, but you could tell. Mike dropped to the ground. As he picked himself up he heard a growl from the stands. He saw Jug Slavin on the step of the dugout, shouting something at Fritz Wesson. Fritz merely took off his cap and smoothed his hair.

Mike knew, for a fact, that Fritz Wesson had thrown at his head. The pitch hadn't been wild; it had been well controlled. He dug his spikes in, brought the bat back parallel with his shoulders, and crouched just slightly. He sighted in as Fritz went into the stretch. The ball came in as he had expected; it was a let-up, on the outside and low. This pitch was a common trick with a dust-off pitcher, and Mike was set for it. He came around on it and met it.

The ball rose on a line and gained altitude as though it were headed for another planet. Koppick, in left field, did not even chase it. He turned and watched its flight with the detached interest of a hunter whose gun jams just as the ducks leave the pond.

There was only one trouble with the blow: it was very close to the foul line. As it described its majestic arc, the plate umpire and the third-base umpire jumped to their battle stations along the foul line and stared hard. There was not the least doubt about the distance the ball would go; this one was due to leave the premises and would probably wind up several blocks away.

Mike was jogging toward second, Madigan had crossed the plate, and Woodward was almost there, when the third-base umpire waved the foul sign— the to-your-bases one—with his right hand.

Everybody in the Blue Sox dugout sprang out, with Jug Slavin leading the pack. Jug headed for the plate umpire, not the third-base umpire. Joining him very quickly was Shanty Milligan, the Clipper manager, and a few of his henchmen from the bench.

It was a clambake. Shanty Milligan and his brood retreated as the plate umpire kept shaking his head no to Jug Slavin. Madigan, with his chin jutting out, was staring into the plate umpire's face. Lasky was trying to push Madigan out of the way so he could have his turn at self-expression. The umpire pulled his watch, and in a few moments the argument was settled. The ball was officially foul. Madigan, Lasky, Slavin, Gibbs, and Walker headed into the tunnel—thumbed out of the game.

Phil Doyle went out to second to run for Madigan. Mike came back to the plate and took his bat from the boy, who was waiting with it.

"Hit 'em right next time," said Berry, the Clipper catcher.

Mike said, "If he throws at my head again—"

"Sue him," Berry said. "Go to court about it."

"I won't go to court about it," Mike said. "I'll go out to the mound about it."

"You do," Berry said, "and I'll be right after you."

"Play ball," the umpire said, as though it pained him—as though he hadn't used the phrase in many years but felt that at this particular moment he really ought to.

Fritz Wesson, standing on the mound, took off his cap and stroked his hair again. He shook off Berry's call with a sharp, horizontal swing of his head. He shook off another one. Then, finally, he nodded.

Fritz delivered. From the moment the ball left his hand, Mike knew it was the duster, all over again. It was even more than a duster; it was an arrow aimed at a bull's-eye.

Mike went down again. Then he jumped up and raced toward the mound, Berry after him, the crowd screaming and on their feet. Fritz Wesson met him midway. Mike swung, and he connected. His fist hit Fritz Wesson somewhere in the middle of his face, and Fritz went down like a poled ox.

Mike was aware that people were holding his arms now, that Wesson was trying to get up and couldn't. He was aware that he was being thrown out of the ball game and that someone was forcibly leading him off the field. The crowd was applauding him as he went into the tunnel and walked under the unshaded electric-light bulbs strung along the ceiling.

In the dressing room Jug Slavin, Johnny Madigan, Eddie Lasky, Pete Gibbs, and Bud Walker were listening to the radio. The broadcaster was saying frantically: " . . . and Brooklyn never had anything like this. This was no ballplayers' fight. This was a replay of the Joe Louis–Max Schmeling fight. This was for blood. I never saw a real fist fight on a ball field until this one. Jaffe hit Wesson so hard it's taking two Clippers to help him off the field. Out in the bull pen. . . ."

Slavin, Madigan, Lasky, and the rest all left the radio when they saw Mike. They grouped around him and kept looking at him without saying anything.

Finally Jug said, "I strongly disapprove of fist fights when a ball game is supposed to be going on.

In this case, I approve. Nobody, but nobody, ever had a better right to hit a man."

Mike couldn't say anything. He was trembling. He went over to the bench in front of his locker and sat down. He suddenly realized that this was the first time he had ever hit anybody in his life—boy or man.

CHAPTER

19

"THE thing is," Luke Bates was saying in their hotel room, "you've taken the job away from me and I'm not mad. Usually I get mad when I lose at anything. But this is different. It had to happen."

It was mid-July now, and Mike had been playing left field almost without interruption since the day the Sox had beaten the Clippers 12–10 and the fist fight had occurred. The Sox had swept the series and had climbed to within one game of first place. Since then the pennant race had been a dogfight: the Sox, the Clippers, and the Redskins all took turns at the top of the league. Right now the Sox were there, a game and a half ahead of the Clippers and two and a half games ahead of the Redskins.

Playing steadily and still hitting fourth, Mike was

batting .357, but he was not in contention for the league batting title, because as yet he hadn't had enough times at bat. He was creeping up, though. There was no doubt about it now—Woodward and Jaffe represented the fiercest one-two punch in the league. Nobody walked Woodward to get at Jaffe.

Mike had begun to think differently since that day when he had completely lost control of himself and walked midway to the mound to slug Fritz Wesson. No matter how you boiled it down, he saw, being a professional baseball player meant that you could not lose—at least, you could not lose gracefully. As an amateur, you could always lose gracefully and be praised for being a good sportsman. But in professional baseball, losing was the real disgrace.

He had thought several times about that crack Stan Davis, the general manager, had made. It had stuck in his craw. "This lad is the sympathetic type. He's just another one of those nice guys." Mike knew the famous remark Davis had had in mind: "Nice guys finish last."

No matter what anyone thought of the man who had made that remark, there was no getting around the fact that, in order to survive, you couldn't give an inch; you couldn't be sympathetic, or easygoing. You had to fight, fight, fight, as the high-school cheerleaders used to put it—but they didn't really know what they were cheering about. Only the pros knew that, the men who were fighting for a bigger salary next year. The amateurs never knew.

Mike thought about Luke Bates. Here was a man who had really been around, who had had just about as honorable a career in baseball as anyone you could name. But Luke Bates, when the chips were down, would cut you in half. It had to be that way. Somehow, the emotional release of smashing Fritz Wesson in the face had changed Mike's whole way of thinking. He knew, too, that his playing every day and his new acceptance by the team also had something to do with the change. He *really* wanted to win now.

There was a knock on the door, and Luke Bates opened it. Ed Daly, the columnist, walked in. Mike had never liked Ed Daly since the day he had written the piece about what was wrong with Mike Jaffe. But then very few ballplayers liked Ed Daly. And as Luke Bates had pointed out, Daly didn't waste his time attacking ballplayers unless he thought they were important.

"Wanted to have a chat," Daly said.

"I've got to write a letter," Mike told him.

"All right," Daly said. "Some other time. You've

been going great. You're playing ball these days, Mike."

"Thanks," Mike said.

"You're putting on weight. It's a good sign."

Luke Bates stood up. "The man has to write a letter."

"I won't bother him," Daly said, and sat down. "You know what a lot of pitchers say about you these days, Mike?"

Mike shook his head.

"They say that even when you go for the bad pitch, you get a hunk of it. You've earned a lot of respect around the league."

"Glad to hear it," Mike said.

"When would it suit you for us to have that chat?"

"What chat?"

"The one I spoke of."

"Oh, any time. Later on."

"How about breakfast tomorrow?"

"I eat early."

"So do I. Let's say about eight tomorrow morning?"

Mike looked toward Luke. Luke nodded slightly. "Sure thing, Mr. Daly," Mike said. "Eight tomorrow. In the coffee shop."

"See you then," Daly said, as he arose.

Mike knew—Luke Bates had drummed it into him —that even when you did not especially care for a sports columnist, you had to give him some of your time when he wanted it. It was part of what the front office called public relations. An interview was free advertising for the club. You couldn't brush it off without depriving the club of valuable and free publicity.

At the door, Ed Daly paused and turned. "By the way, one of the things I wanted to talk to you about was the news about Fritz Wesson. Maybe you haven't heard it. It just came in on the wire service at the office."

Mike said, "What about Fritz Wesson?"

"The Clippers asked for waivers on him. Nobody picked them up, so they gave him his outright release. I understand he's signed with a Double-A club, somewhere down South."

"I didn't know about that," Mike said.

Daly said, "See you in the morning."

Mike turned to Luke as the door closed. "You don't think," he said, "because I hit him that day. . . ."

"He was on his way out," Luke said. Then he added, "Probably."

CHAPTER

20

THE news about Fritz Wesson bothered Mike. He knew that it shouldn't, that if the same thing happened all over again, he would probably wind up being just as enraged and doing just the same thing. Wesson had asked for it, not just that day, but on many previous occasions. Still, it looked as though that day had brought Fritz Wesson's big-league pitching career to an end. Fritz wasn't young but he wasn't old, either—thirty-two.

Mike learned, from his conversation with Ed Daly at breakfast the next morning—as well as from what he read in the papers later—that Fritz Wesson hadn't been waived down to the minors because of any disability resulting from Mike's punch, even though it had been an extremely powerful blow.

"The guy," said Daly, "just got a slightly bent beak, which was straightened out quickly enough. But he'd been getting along by frightening batters with that bean-ball stuff, and you took the fear out of the other batters in the league, because you frightened Wesson. All of a sudden he didn't have the nerve to use his duster on a long-ball hitter. And all of a sudden he was getting tagged with so many home runs that every manager figured he was too big a risk with men on the bases."

"I see," Mike said.

He didn't really. He plunged into his oatmeal and cream while Daly sipped tomato juice. Perhaps if Fritz Wesson hadn't been the first person he had ever hit with his fist in his life, he would have thought less about the whole thing. He knew that ballplayers who were unwilling to fight when the situation called for it did not earn respect from other ballplayers. He supposed, in a way, that he had earned the team's respect that day; actually, everything he had seen and read about in the papers ever since proved it. And the fact that he now played left field every day, while Luke Bates sat on the bench except for occasional pinch-hitting duties . . . that was certainly the final proof. But justified or not, it bothered him that he had damaged the career of a good pitcher—more than damaged it. It looked now as though he had just about ended it.

"You're a funny kid," Daly said.

Mike looked at him in a puzzled way.

"I mean," Daly said, "and that's why I wanted to talk to you last night—everybody is impressed by you except one person."

"You," Mike said, remembering Daly's early column about him.

"No, *you*."

The waitress arrived and picked up Mike's empty oatmeal bowl and Daly's tomato-juice glass. Then she deposited a plate of ham steak and four eggs, with four slices of toast, in front of Mike. She also brought a pint of milk and a glass. Daly followed his juice with a cup of black coffee.

Mike cut into the ham steak. "If you don't think that I think I'm a pretty good ballplayer, then you're wrong, Mr. Daly."

"You're backing up what I said," Daly said. "You described yourself just then as a 'pretty good ball-player.' Don't you ever read what the sports writers write about you?"

"I read something you wrote once that I didn't like," Mike said. "The time when I first came back from the Blues, or a little after, and broke up that no-hitter of Milt Greene's."

"Eat your ham and eggs," Daly said. "We'll talk later."

It all turned out, as far as Mike could figure it, that what Daly wanted out of him in the way of a story—and he had learned that sports writers thought they were wasting their time if they didn't get a story out of you—was whether he was in any way affected emotionally by Fritz Wesson's release. When this fact sank in, Mike said even less than he was in the habit of saying. So it was practically a wasted morning for Daly.

When the interview was over, Daly said, "Well, thanks, Mike. You haven't told me a thing, but I appreciate your giving me your time."

"I was in no hurry," Mike said. "It was a good breakfast."

"I have no story," Daly said, "but I'm beginning to think you're my favorite ballplayer."

Mike still felt slightly puzzled as he watched Daly walk across the hotel lobby after they had parted outside the coffee shop.

That afternoon, in the final game of a three-game series the Sox were playing with the Grays, a funny thing happened. It was a new experience to Mike: he got a riding from the opposite bench. When he started out for left field, he heard voices directed his way from the Grays' bench.

"There he goes, the Mauler!"

"If he can't bat 'em out of there, he'll bruise 'em out of there!"

"Big Jab Jaffe!"

Mike guessed the yells must refer to the news about Fritz Wesson. Nothing like this had ever happened to him before. He slowed his trot as he went out to his position, straining to hear more. He was not used to being jockeyed from the bench, and he could not figure why it had suddenly started.

It unsettled him a little. At least, it seemed like that. The lead-off man for the Grays hit one to left, and he started in on it. Then he realized he should have instantly started back. He leaped high, after he had reversed his course, but the ball went off his finger tips. It hit the base of the left-field wall. He couldn't seem to corral it and the lead-off man, who was fast, wound up with a sliding triple on what Mike knew should have been an out. Not an easy one, but an out.

The runner scored a moment later on a ground ball that went behind the bag at second. Walker reached it, whirled, and turned the play into an out. But the run was a bad beginning for the Sox and for Mike.

Now that the Grays were convinced he listened to the bench jockeying, they kept it up. Mike batted in the first inning, after two outs and a double by Woodward. The first pitch low-bridged him. He went down. He was surprised, but not angry. He had made up his mind he would not lose his head over such a pitch again. Ball one.

The remarks from the Grays' bench somehow found their way to his ears. Before the next pitch came in, straight and fast, Mike was listening. That was strike one. There was another pitch dangerously close to his head, and he dropped. The Sox bench started yelling, but Mike said nothing. He didn't even think of making a protest.

"One-punch Jaffe," said Charlie Dixon, the Grays' catcher.

Mike just set himself silently for the next pitch.

"A preliminary boy, that's all," Dixon said.

There was no word from Mike. The ball poured in, and he swung. It wasn't as fast as he had expected. It went sky-high to deep short and was taken easily. The pop-up could have happened to anyone and had happened to him before. It probably would happen again. What bothered him was his feeling of uncertainty. He had taken two dusters, or semi-dusters at least, and had not wanted to do anything or say anything.

When he went near the dugout to get his glove, which the bat boy tossed to him, Jug Slavin was standing in front. "You let a pitcher get away with that once more," Jug called, "and the word will be around the league fast."

Mike didn't even nod toward Jug. The remark had been made in a very low voice, so no one else except the bat boy could have heard it, he was sure. He jogged out to left field with a feeling that Jug was angrier at the pitcher than he was. He knew this wasn't good.

CHAPTER
21

IN EARLY August the Blue Sox went into Clipper Stadium for a double-header and two single games. They had managed to push themselves to the top of the heap in the past few weeks, but they were leading the Clippers by only a game and a half. The double-header came up on the first day, and both clubs had worked out their pitching rotation so that their top pitchers were ready to go.

It was Lasky and Hanson for the Sox, of course; Rodriguez would pitch the third game and Harry Diefendorf the final. The Clippers were using Wilcy Lord, their top left-hander, in the first game of the double-header, and Rob Hurley, a fast-balling right-hander, in the second. The Stadium wasn't filled; it held 52,000 officially and at game time only 51,328 tickets had been sold.

As the groundkeepers dragged the mats around the infield and the managers conferred at the plate with the umpires about the ground rules—rules they had all known by heart for years and years—Jocko Tyler, the TV play-by-play broadcaster, was saying into his microphone, "The vital mark of the Sox, of all real champs, is that ability to knock off the contender when they reach hand-to-hand combat with him. They have a supreme confidence in themselves, a confidence that goes way back to the early days of Jug Slavin's management. In those days Madigan was a rookie and Marty Blake was on first; Augie Marshall was in right field, Vic Valenti in center, Tweet Tillman behind the plate. Time and time again, season after season, they have risen up to flatten the one team they had to flatten. Last year it was the Redskins, whom they beat fourteen out of twenty-two games. If the Redskins had been able to reverse that count, or even break even, they could have played in the World Series, instead of the Sox. Today the same test faces the Sox once more. There go the Clippers out on the field. . . ."

Inside the Sox dugout Jug Slavin was making some final remarks, and they were all addressed to

[148]

Mike Jaffe, in the privacy of the far corner. "I can tell you right now," Jug said, "that before this game is over you will be dusted. Brushed back, as pitchers like to call it."

"That doesn't bother me any," Mike said.

"I know it doesn't. And by now the whole league knows it doesn't. Ever since the day the Clippers released Wesson, you've been taking the dusters as politely as a sick patient takes his doctor's pills. The Clippers will be on you."

"I already said, that's all right with me," Mike told him.

"And I'm telling you, it's *not* all right with me. One, yes. That can happen. Two, no. That's deliberate. Especially when the pitcher is working on a clean-up hitter with men on the bases. Your RBI record has slumped badly, ever since that day we played the Grays and you took those bean balls lying down."

"How can I act mad if I don't feel mad?" Mike demanded. "A pitcher has to protect his earned-run average any way he can."

"So help me," Jug said. "After all this time you're still on the side of the pitchers."

"I shouldn't have hit Wesson that day. I was sorry afterward."

"Why?"

"He's smaller than I am."

"He could have killed you if you hadn't had twenty-year-old reflexes. Did you ever stop to think of that?"

"Got to get a drink of water," Mike said, and walked over to the cooler.

Wilcy Lord, though a left-hander, was primarily a control pitcher who worked the corners. He worked the corners on Madigan with two pitches in succession, so Madigan took no further chances. He splashed the third pitch, thrown to him on the outside, toward right field. It was a looper. Richman back of second, Mansell in center, and Bower in right all converged. It looked as though no one would get it, even though it was as soft as a pop fly. Madigan, the opportunist, never slowed down as he rounded first, and it was clear that he would make two bases on it unless a minor miracle occurred.

The minor miracle came to pass. Bower lunged and wound up on the grass like an inexpert diver who has made a belly whopper off the springboard. But he gloved it and he held on to it.

Madigan came back into the dugout growling. "I wouldn't mind being robbed that way, except that

Bower is an old man. He should take better care of himself."

Fiske swung hard on the first pitch and lofted the ball deep to right. Usually, however, Fiske got most of his hits with line drives, not lofts. This one went close to the rim of the right-field bleachers, but it didn't reach them—and Bower did. That was two outs.

Woodward, batting right-handed, took two balls and then a strike. He caught the fourth pitch just where the curve broke, and it skimmed over Mac-Donald's head, at short, into left center for a clean single.

As Mike stepped in, he heard Berry say, "Hello, one-punch. I hear you ran out of little guys to slug and have hung up the gloves."

"You don't make me laugh much," Mike said.

"It must be you," Berry said. "I always roll 'em in the aisles."

Mike took a ball, low and outside. The next pitch was high, but he saw that Woodward was off and running, with a good jump on the ball, so he swung at it to help protect him. Berry's throw was good, but Woodward had too much of a start and was too fast. He made it.

Mike promptly slammed the next one into left

center. It felt like two bases when it left his bat; but Mansell, in center, was a rabbit. He cut it off with a backhanded sweep of his glove and, halfway to second, Mike retreated. At least, he had driven in Woodward with the game's first run.

That was all for the Sox, but the run began to look big, the way Lasky was going. By the top of the seventh the score was still 1-0 in favor of the Sox, and no Clipper runner had managed to get beyond second base. Still, it was anybody's ball game. And then, in the seventh inning, the Sox came up with a chance to break it wide open.

Walker led off by striking out, but Lasky reached first on a Baltimore chop that bounced so high it seemed to hang in the air like a toy balloon filled with gas. Madigan got another cheap one, a slow roller between third and short that he beat out for a leg hit. Men on first and second now. Fiske hit a ground ball that had little to recommend it except that it moved slowly toward first and while he was tagged out on the line, going down, the runners moved on to second and third.

Berry and Shanty Milligan went out to the mound to talk to Lord. There wasn't the slightest doubt in the minds of any of the fifty-odd thousand persons inside the Stadium as to what they were discussing.

Mike knew that this had always been the spot where Woodward was given the intentional pass, before he had come up. Since then, it hadn't happened so often. At first, not at all. Lately, once in a while.

Mike remained kneeling in the on-deck circle as Milligan returned to the bench and Berry to his position behind the plate. Then he got a pretty good picture of how his rating around the league had started to slip. Lord threw four wide ones to Woodward to load the bases, showing that the Clippers preferred to take their chances with Mike Jaffe these days, even with the bases full in a one-run ball game.

Berry greeted him gleefully. "The vote at the mound was three to nothing to pitch to Jaffe."

"That suits me," Mike said.

"Got your protective helmet on?" Berry asked.

Mike saw, on the first pitch, that what Jug Slavin had said to him in the dugout before the game was true. "Before this game is over," Jug had said, "you will be dusted." Well, no matter what Lord tried to do, eventually he would have to pitch to him. Lord wouldn't walk in a run in a game that was 1-0 in the seventh, if he could help it. And with the control that Lord had shown today, he most certainly could help it.

The first pitch was the warning flash. It came in hard and high and close to his head. Mike went down. As he picked himself up, he was aware of an angry racket in the Sox dugout.

"Had enough?" Berry said.

The umpire called time. He stepped in front of the plate and said something to Lord, who met him midway. There wasn't much doubt, either, in any-one's mind as to what the umpire was telling Lord. Lord spread his hands in a gesture of baffled in-nocence. Now the Clipper bench was yelling at the umpire, while the men on the Sox bench mega-phoned remarks toward Lord through their cupped hands.

Lord, as if to prove his innocence—to prove he was merely pitching high and inside because he con-sidered that the batter's weakness—threw another one high and inside. But this one was a breaking curve, slightly less than shoulder-high, and Mike watched it go by for strike one. One and one now.

The third pitch was the first pitch all over again, and again Mike dove. When he got up this time he felt the rage that he had felt for Fritz Wesson. He took three steps toward the mound, fists clenched. Then, as he squinted at Lord, it struck him how small the man was, at least three or four inches shorter than he was. And not stocky, almost skinny-looking.

Mike's rage suddenly evaporated. He turned back to the batter's box and started to bat the dust from his pants, his head down. He heard the crowd jeering, saw Lord laughing at him, and as he turned he saw Jug Slavin coming out of the dugout, waving his arms.

Then as the umpire called time and Jug headed toward him, he saw, to his utter astonishment, a second figure emerging from the Sox dugout. It was Luke Bates, fumbling at the bat rack. Jug spoke briefly to the umpire, who turned toward the press box and pointed at Mike and Luke Bates in turn. Bates was advancing toward the plate as Mike stood there, staring, completely dumbfounded. Jug was beckoning to him. He could not believe it, but from the amplifiers he heard the booming of the official announcement: "Luke Bates batting for Jaffe. Bates . . ."

CHAPTER

22

THE next morning Mike slept later than usual; in fact, he slept later than he felt like sleeping. But he had fought against waking up, remembering something vaguely about yesterday that he did not wish to think about yet. Mike did what most people do in that situation: he rolled over in bed and went back to sleep.

His sleep lasted for a while, but eventually he had to sit up in bed, had to think about what it was he didn't want to think about. Then he remembered quickly. He stalled the thinking processes by looking over at the other twin bed and discovering, not much to his surprise, that Luke Bates had already arisen and gone down to breakfast.

Mike got up and sat on the side of his bed, rubbing his fingers through his hair. He yawned, looked out the window, and saw some other windows and a murky haze in between. He put one foot on top of the other, scratched the side of his head, then looked down at the floor.

That was when Mike saw the newspaper. The hotel left the morning paper at each door as a hospitable service. Mike picked it up and glanced at it. Crumpled though it was, the headline on the page which faced him—the sports page—was plain. In large black type it said: "Sox Sweep Two from Clippers, 1-0, 3-1."

The crumpled state of the newspaper told him that Luke had read it before leaving the room. He did not think it any accident that Luke had left it there, staring up at him. Apparently Luke had wanted him to read it. He did.

With practically no batting attack behind them, the two aces of the Blue Sox mound staff handcuffed the Clippers yesterday afternoon to go ahead three and one half games in the pennant race, their biggest margin of the year. The scores were 1-0 and 3-1, in that order. Eddie Lasky pitched the shutout opener, giving up only four hits, while Bix Hanson applied the crusher in the afterpiece, allowing five hits. This was a thoroughly aroused Sox team, and what they lacked in power they made up for with grimly tight defensive play.

The Sox drove through to the double sweep after Jug Slavin, in obvious anger, made a most unusual managerial move. With bases loaded in the top of the seventh, as a result of two cheap hits by Lasky and Madigan and an intentional walk to Woodward after Fiske had advanced both runners with a sacrifice, Mike Jaffe had a chance to put the game away.

Wilcy Lord then threw one close to Jaffe's head. The word has been passed around the league that you can knock Jaffe down these days, keep him from digging in, and get no argument about it. It turned out that way. The Sox bench got steamed up about it, but Jaffe didn't. He took a strike and then Lord knocked him down again. Jaffe got up, started to go out to the mound, but slapped the dirt off his pants instead.

Jug Slavin had had enough. At this point, he dramatically lifted his .348 clean-up hitter for an aging .291 hitter, Luke Bates. Bates faced Lord, looking as angry as Jaffe had not. He belted the first pitch, a line drive that looked like a bases-clearing stand-up triple, but somehow Mansell raced fast enough to his right to make the finest leaping catch seen around this ball lot all year.

From that incident on, the Sox looked unbeatable. Their pitching was superb and their defense was so tight that it was heartbreaking for the Clipper fans to watch. The second game was settled in the fifth inning when Woodward slammed one into the upper deck in right field with two men on.

Bates played left field in the second game too, batting sixth while Stookey moved to the clean-up spot. Bates failed to get a hit all day, but his defensive play sparkled and his hustle was evident in every move he made. Jaffe was not even visible on the Sox bench, and it was learned after the game that Slavin had suspended him for three days, which means that he will see no further action in this all-important four-game series.

Mike could read no more of it. He felt angry, really angry, and all this anger was directed toward Jug Slavin. He was going to see Slavin now, this morning, and let it out of his system. He was suspended for what? For not acting like a rowdy? Slavin had always made a big point of wanting gentlemen on his ball club, not rowdies. What he had done to Mike, as far as Mike was concerned, did not make sense.

He got dressed and went down to the lobby. The coffee shop, a quick look showed him, was clear of ballplayers. Just a few civilians, as Tweet Tillman always referred to people who did not play ball, still remained. He hurriedly had juice and a bowl of cereal, nothing more. It was the first time he hadn't been hungry for breakfast that he could re-member. But he wasn't hungry this morning.

Back in the lobby he looked around to see if he could spot Slavin. There was no sign of him. He saw Madigan and Fiske sitting on a leather lounge across the way. The two smallest regulars of the Sox always seemed to pal around together. He went over to them.

As soon as they looked up, Mike knew that he was no longer one of them, not the way he had been. Their gaze was cool, not unfriendly exactly, but not friendly either. It was sort of speculative, as though they were meeting a stranger for the first time and sizing him up to his disadvantage.

"You seen Slavin around?" he asked.

Madigan shook his head. "Not in the last half hour, no."

"Maybe he went to his room," Mike said.

"I don't think he did," Fiske said.

"Oh? You mean he went out somewhere?"

Fiske looked at Madigan, and Madigan looked at Fiske, and then both of them glanced back appraisingly at Mike. "He went up in the elevator," Madigan explained. "But I don't think he went to *his* room, because he was with the G.M., Davis."

"Davis?" Mike said. "I didn't know he was here."

"He wasn't," Fiske said. "Only he flew in this morning. He must have had something on his mind, I guess."

"You know how those G.M.'s are," Madigan added.

CHAPTER
23

CHIP FISKE'S surmise that Stan Davis must have had something on his mind had been one hundred per cent correct. In a suite on the fifteenth floor of the hotel, he was telling Jug Slavin about it in no uncertain terms, right at that moment. He had his coat and tie off and his sleeves rolled up, despite the suite's air-conditioned comfort. He was, as usual, stalking around and looking very fierce, with his brow deeply furrowed. The expression on his face resembled that of a fullback about to plunge through the center of the line for the game-winning yardage.

"I don't know what rocked me harder—Simple Simon Jaffe taking two knockdowns and acting polite about it, or you suspending him for the rest of the series."

"Who won the double-header?" Jug inquired.

"Don't get bright with me," Davis said.

"Well, to put it in a dumb way then," Jug said, "after I saw from the bench what you saw on television, I knew I was through with Jaffe. Not just for three days, but for the rest of my life, if he wants it that way."

Davis looked out the window as though contemplating a jump through it. "Just like that, eh?" he said. "You can get .348 long-ball hitters any time you want, I guess."

"I won't get another hitter like Jaffe in five years, maybe ten," Jug said. "But at the same time, he doesn't add up. Not with this team. Not with *my* kind of team."

"You better spell this out for me," Davis told him. "I'm groping to find a few stray grains of sense in what you're saying."

Jug proceeded to expound the Jaffe problem as he saw it. He pointed out first that in the beginning, when Mike had balked at converting, Davis had had no patience while he himself had said that Mike couldn't be forced into it, he had to want to do it.

"So he *did* want to do it finally," Davis said.

"So he *didn't*. He came back here from the Blues feeling horsewhipped. He said, and he was right, that if he didn't agree he would simply be shipped down and down. We both know you and your front office would have done exactly that."

Davis, who was not a man to contest an obvious truth, said nothing.

"As a result," Jug said, "what came back to us was a Jaffe who was just going along, playing the front-office game with the front office. But his heart wasn't in it."

"How about the day he slugged that what's-his-name—Wesson?"

Jug nodded. "That was a good sign. You know I don't approve of fist fights among ballplayers, but this one was justified, and it looked to me as though Jaffe had started to think like a hitter, not like a pitcher."

"I was sure of it," Davis said.

"But when Wesson was waived out, after that incident, then Mike was flooded with remorse. Look. Suppose you had a fight with your brother. If you hurt your brother in that fight—no matter how angry or right you were—you'd still feel dead wrong after it was over."

"See what you mean," Davis said.

"I can't afford to have a man with his gentle attitude toward pitchers hitting in the most im-

portant spot in my batting order, day after day.
Pitchers are still his blood brothers."

"Suppose we sell him to the Clippers, for in-
stance," Davis pointed out. "He'll probably beat our
brains out."

"I don't propose to sell him to anybody during the
winter," Jug said.

"What do you propose to do then?"

"Simply do what he asked for in the first place:
give him his wish and let him renounce playing in
the outfield forever. He can go down to the Blues
again and return to his pitching."

"You call that a solution?"

"No," Jug said, "but I think it's the only way *to*
a solution, if there really is a solution to Jaffe. Remember—he was conditioned from the cradle to
believe he was a pitcher. Everything else seems
unimportant to him."

Davis finally quit stalking and sat down. "And
we go along with Bates and hope to win the pennant?"

"Yes," Jug said. "Unless the right thing happens
this time. Unless Mike Jaffe wants to come back to
us of his own free will, with pitching out of his mind,
with his heart set on being the best hitter in the
league—which he can be, I think. In Jaffe we could

have the best right-handed slugger that anyone has seen in a long, long time. But right now he's a drag on this team and I don't care about averages or RBI's or power to left. That's my thinking on this matter."

Davis stood up and walked over to the window. Once more he seemed to be considering the pleasant possibility of jumping through it. Davis had the reputation of being the shrewdest general manager in baseball. Now he bowed to Jug Slavin. "O.K., Skip," he said, and his calling Jug by that name was an acknowledgment that Jug was in charge of the Jaffe crisis. "You have it your way. I'll go along. I expect nothing. But I'll go along."

"I expect nothing either," Jug said. "All I expect is that three years from now Mike Jaffe will be pitching for a Class B club somewhere in Georgia, waiting to get the call to replace the aging Lasky."

"You won't take him the way he is, .348 batting average and all?"

"I'll take a .200 batter over him, and pitchers don't even knock down the .200 boys."

"Give the lad the word then," Davis said.

"Right away," Jug assured him.

CHAPTER
24

"RIGHT away" turned out to be the exact phrase for it. When Jug got off the elevator, at the lobby floor, he saw Mike standing at the hotel entrance looking out at the passing traffic in the street.

Mike, by now, was boiling inside. He had figured everything out even more thoroughly than he had earlier, in his room. He was being punished, publicly humiliated, for not being a brawler. And Jug Slavin had gone on record as not wanting a brawler on his team! He was trying to be an outfielder for the Sox when he wanted to be a pitcher. He was doing a good job of it as far as he could see. His work in the field, he knew, was not outstanding, but it was not sloppy. His hitting was more powerful than that of any other player in the line-up except

Russ Woodward. All Mike wanted was a face-to-face talk with Jug Slavin at once.

His wish was promptly granted. He felt a tap on his shoulder and when he turned around, there stood Jug Slavin. "Want to talk to you, Mike," Jug said.

"Me too," Mike said.

"Let's go into the coffee shop," Jug suggested.

They went in and sat down. Jug ordered coffee while Mike ordered a malted. When they had been served, Jug said, "Mike, I've got an apology to make to you."

Mike stared at him. He could hardly believe what he had heard. For a big-league manager to apologize to a twenty-year-old rookie whom he had just suspended was practically unbelievable. All the anger went right out of Mike. The only conclusion he could make was that he had misjudged the manager, after all. Jug had made a mistake in removing him from the game and plastering a suspension on him, and he was willing to admit his mistake.

Mike sucked on the straw but hardly tasted the malted.

Jug said, "I apologize for trying to make you convert to the outfield. You've convinced me you're a pitcher at heart, always will be, and always should be."

This admission threw Mike completely. He thought it over, twisted it around, and tried to figure out what would come next.

"I'm so convinced that you are right and I am wrong," Jug went on, "that I'm going to reverse my field entirely. You can quit left field and start pitching again."

"Well!" Mike said. "I mean, I'm ready. I've been warming up every day in my spare time with Artie, the bat boy. With anybody who would catch me. I can pitch for you any time, Mr. Slavin. You just give me the chance."

"I'm giving you that chance, Mike," Jug Slavin said. "Not with the Sox, of course. There's no room for you here on the pitching staff."

"Oh?" Mike said. The question came out of his mouth in a way that gave it a sort of hollow sound.

"Naturally not," Jug said. "You knew, when we brought you back from the Blues, that we weren't bringing you back as a pitcher. But I think it's only right that you have a chance to prove yourself at what you really want to do—pitch."

"That's . . . great, Mr. Slavin."

"Now the thing to bear in mind," Jug said, "is that nobody in the front office is going to shove you down and down in the classifications. I've just discussed that point with Mr. Davis, and he agrees with me that the best thing all around is for you to forget about everything except pitching."

"That's . . . mighty nice of you and Mr. Davis," Mike said.

"And also," Jug said, "forget about the Sox for the time being. A few years of grooming, and you may be back with us. Right now we've got a pennant to win. I've got to concentrate on that."

"Sure," Mike said. "But Mr. Slavin—"

Jug raised his right hand, palm forward. "You're a free man, Mike. You're rid of us. I'll speak to Burt Kelly, and he'll get you going this afternoon. Give my regards to Pops Medlicott. I'll see that he gives you every opportunity. Next spring we'll look you over in our rookie school at Glensota."

"Mr. Slavin—"

Jug arose. He had signed the check that the waitress had left. He said, "Don't thank me, Mike. Thank Mr. Davis. We want you to do what makes you happy."

"Well . . . thanks," Mike said. He felt all mixed up. He had been prepared for several different outcomes of his conversation with Jug Slavin, but not this. Yet he was being given the opportunity he had always wanted. He was free of the feeling that he had to do what the front office told him to do. He had finally won his fight with them. But it suddenly struck him that leaving the Blue Sox for the Blues was a little like leaving the Waldorf for a firetrap hotel down around the Bowery.

Mike called after Jug, "What about my suspension? Does it mean I can't play for the Blues for three days, or—"

"It's lifted," Jug said. "I'll make that official at once. Good luck, kid. I've got to get out to the park. We're in first place and that's where we're going to stay. Got to beat it."

Mike started to follow him. "Do you know where Burt Kelly is?" he asked.

"Oh," Jug said. "Burt may be at the park by now. But you have to go out, anyway, to pick up your stuff. See him there."

Mike nodded.

"See you in the spring," Jug said. "At the rookie camp. See if you can sharpen that slider. It might help a little."

MIKE went to the visitors' dressing room at Clipper Stadium to get his belongings from his locker. Everything that had happened here depressed him. He couldn't understand it. He had won his fight, he was free to do what he had always wanted to do, and he should have felt triumphant. But he didn't. He thought, instead, as he entered the room, that this might be the last time he would see the inside of a big-league dressing room.

The reaction of the ballplayers who had got there ahead of him depressed him even more. He realized, by what they said, that they already knew he was leaving them. They seemed completely indifferent.

Gibbs walked by as Mike was pulling stuff out of

his locker and jamming it haphazardly into his suit-case. "Good luck down there, kid," Gibbs said.

Mike looked up. "Thanks," he said, but Gibbs had already moved on. He hadn't paused to chat, the way he usually did.

Pickles, the clubhouse man, came over. "Need any help on anything?" he asked halfheartedly.

"All I need is to get hold of Burt Kelly," Mike said.

"I'll tell him. He's around somewhere. Happy landings." Pickles walked off.

Mike continued to push things into his suitcase. He came across his old glove—his pitcher's glove, with the shorter, stubbier fingers for handling ground balls better. It was badly in need of lub-rication, he saw. But he wasn't going to take care of that just now. He wanted to get out—as fast as he possibly could.

Jug Slavin came out of his office, glanced across the room toward him, and just nodded as he went on his way.

Artie, the bat boy, stopped and spoke to him. "You really going down again, Mike?" Artie asked.

Mike nodded.

"You really going to quit hitting? I mean, try pitching again?"

"I was always a pitcher, Artie," Mike explained.

[173]

"Playing left field was just an experiment."

Artie shook his head. ".348!" he said, and whistled softly. "Some experiment. Well, maybe you'll be back. Who knows?" Even Artie walked off.

Mike saw Burt Kelly, the road secretary, coming into the room. Jug Slavin spoke to him, and Kelly nodded quickly. Then Kelly came over to Mike. "I can get you a plane flight this afternoon," Kelly said. "You might as well get there as fast as you can."

"I don't like flying much," Mike said, "when I don't have to."

"Have it your way," Kelly said. "You'll be on a sleeper then. Probably leave in the early evening. Stick around awhile and I'll let you know."

"I don't like those upper berths much," Mike said.

Kelly raised his eyebrows. "Down where you're going you'll be glad to get one—glad you're not traveling by bus."

Mike had everything packed. He heard the clatter of spikes all around him as the Sox players finished dressing, one by one, and trooped out to the tunnel that led to the field. He took his bag over to Pickles and said, "I'll leave this with you, Pickles. I have to wait around until Mr. Kelly tells me about my train reservation."

Pickles took it, saying nothing.

"Tell Mr. Kelly, if he's looking for me, that I went up to the press box for a while, to kill time. I'll be back soon."

Pickles nodded.

As Mike started to leave, Luke Bates caught up with him. Luke slapped him on the back and shook hands with him when he turned around. "You're making one awful mistake, kid," Luke said. "But it's your mistake to make."

"I won my fight with the front office," he said. "That's more than most ballplayers can say."

"Well, here's one ballplayer who just wants to win a pennant. *And* stay in the big leagues. Everything except the big leagues is nothing. I found that out. You'll find it out."

"I'll be back," Mike said. "On my terms. As a pitcher."

Luke shook his head. "I'll miss the sight of you, Mike, just taking one of those cuts of yours at a baseball. Well, you're only twenty . . . plenty of time to mend your fences."

Luke went out, and Mike headed down the long concrete cave under the stands and up the concrete ramp to the second tier. There were only a few fans there as early as this; most of them were boys with baseball gloves, trying to catch foul balls during the practice. Just before he reached the circular stairway that led to the press box and the broadcasting booths suspended behind home plate, one of the boys recognized him.

"Hey!" he yelled to another boy. "There goes Mike Jaffe!"

"Yeah!" the other kid yelled back. "I almost didn't recognize him. Only time I ever see him, he's lyin' on the ground."

Mike felt the back of his neck getting warm. The attendant guarding the circular stairway recognized him and passed him in. "Nobody here yet," he said.

"I just want to kill a little time," Mike explained.

The press box, as the attendant had said, was totally deserted. There were a few typewriters, cases still locked tight, along the curving aisles of planked workbenches at which the sports writers made their notes and sometimes wrote their stories when the game was over. Mike sat down in front, staring at the scene before him.

It was a beautiful baseball day—glinting sunshine and blue sky with white clouds floating in it. Reserve players and pitchers not due to pitch roamed the bright green outfield grass. They lazily caught

that's three and a half games out in front? And leaving a .348 batting average behind you?"

"I know what I'm doing," Mike said. "Even if it doesn't look like it right now, to some people."

"Did you ever stop to think," Daly said, "how many assorted ballplayers scattered all over the country are fighting tooth and nail for the very opportunity you've tossed over your shoulder?"

Mike stood up. "I've got to go now, Mr. Daly."

"If there's anything you'd like to say to the Blue Sox fans, you tell me and I'll tell them for you."

Mike thought a minute. Finally he said, "Tell them I thought they treated me great. And I'll be back."

"Pitching or hitting, Mike?"

"Pitching," Mike said.

CHAPTER
26

"WELL, Mike, so you're back with us," Pops Medlicott said, when he showed up in the Blues' clubhouse.

"Yes, Pops," Mike said. "I'm back."

"And you want to pitch again, so they tell me."

"Not again, Pops," Mike said. "Still."

"Well, you'll get every chance. They told me to give you every chance, so thank them, not me."

"I was surprised," Mike said, "when they finally came around to my way of thinking."

"You can use the same locker," Pops said.

Mike didn't think Pops was too cordial, although Pops never said or did anything sharp, anything that hurt. Some of the Blues whom he knew came over—Bob Cosier, Carl Perutz, Slick Hammill.

[180]

"Hello, dope," Cosier said.

"Put a capital *D* on that," Perutz said.

Slick Hammill held out his hand. "Congrats, chum. You showed 'em."

"We had it out," Mike said. "They finally saw it my way." Even as he said it he was thinking what he'd been thinking most of the way out on the train. If, at the last moment, somebody—Jug or Davis—had asked him to change his mind, he might have done so. He hadn't really wanted to leave when it was time to go. But he couldn't swallow his pride and tell them he wanted to stay, after all, and do what they had demanded of him.

Mike looked around the dressing room and already he was assailed by pangs. He was bedded down now in second-rate quarters. He was used to having everything first-rate. He knew he had forced himself to come back here; certainly no one else had made him do it. But here he was. And here he would stay . . . nobody knew how long—years, possibly. Slick Hammill was also big-league material, and he was anchored here.

"You must be a little bit sorry," Cosier said. "You *must* be."

"What do you mean?"

"Listen," Cosier said. "The only reason any of us

are still breathing around here is because we hope we'll get called up, the way you were."

"And also," Perutz said, "we hope we'll be able to hit maybe .284—not .348."

"You did right, kid," Hammill said. "I thought for a while you weren't paying any attention to all the things I used to tell you."

Mike looked at him. "I didn't, too much," he said.

"Then what are you doing back here?" Hammill demanded.

"What I did, I figured out myself," Mike told him.

Cosier looked at Perutz and jerked his thumb at Hammill. "This guy here with the master brain needs to have it retreaded."

"He needed that a long time ago," Perutz said.

Hammill turned on them. "You guys," he said, "were never even up there. You shouldn't speak until you're spoken to."

"Come off it," Cosier said.

"Turn blue," Perutz said.

"Don't pay any attention to these guys," Slick Hammill said to Mike. "You can't even call them has-beens. They never were."

Mike turned and walked away to see about a uniform. That kind of talk made him feel a little ill. You never heard it in the Blue Sox dressing room. How could a team expect to be a team, or win a pennant, when they insulted each other that way? The only thing that made him feel good, at that moment, was his distaste for such petty, mean remarks. It dawned on him that he was thinking big-league, not bush.

Mike asked to pitch batting practice and Pops Medlicott let him. "You're probably rusty," Pops said. "You haven't pitched since early in the season."

"I'm not rusty," Mike said. "I've been working out all the time. I knew my chance would come. I could pitch today if you wanted me to."

Pops cleared his throat. "My rotation is set. Maybe day after tomorrow, or the next day. We'll see."

"Any time you say, Pops," Mike told him. "I'll be ready."

Four days later, on the final day of the Blues' home stand, he got his chance. It was a Sunday double-header and he pitched the first game. The crowd was big, because, of course, the local papers had run several stories about the strange case of a big-leaguer with a .348 average returning to the minors through his own wish. Mike discovered, however, that he was not considered a hero, but a freak. He thought this crowd would be glad to have him back. If they were they didn't show it; they hooted at him.

Mike heard the gibes while he was warming up near the stands, on the first-base side.

"Yoo-hoo!" somebody yelled, in a mocking falsetto voice. "Will you pitch for our softball team when you wash out here?"

"Too good for the big leagues!" another voice shouted.

"He came home to Mother!"

"Just a boy who got separated from the men!"

The remarks stung. He couldn't close his ears to them. Pops Medlicott wasn't batting him clean-up now. He was batting him in the pitcher's usual spot, ninth. The parades were over for Mike Jaffe, in this town. The fans were treating him almost like a kid playing hooky from school.

He hadn't expected this. He had thought this crowd would be all for him. On the return trip he had pictured himself, in his private dream world, as a sort of home-coming hero, a martyr to his principles. But the only welcome he had received had come from Slick Hammill, whom he now knew he despised as a waster of his own talents, a sour and bitter old man before his time. He wanted none of Slick Hammill's adulation, which wasn't adulation at all, but just a sort of misery-loves-company bond.

The first hitter who faced him swung at a fast one and missed it cleanly. He took a second one that shaved a corner. Mike felt he had him on the hook, but after letting a waste pitch go by, the guy hit one off the end of the bat, a feeble thing. However, it ballooned its unimpressive way to short center field and dropped in front of the fielder's outstretched glove for a flabby but clean single.

"Send him out to left field!" somebody shrilled.

"*This* is a pitcher?" someone else screamed.

Mike knew already that the home crowd was solidly against him; they had no sympathy for his return. As a left fielder, they had loved him. As a pitcher, they were telling him to go get lost.

He stretched and fired to the second hitter. This one, a lefty, smashed the ball far out to right. Mike's right fielder leaped and pulled it in—a brilliant play that saved the situation. The third man slapped a grounder down to Cosier, at third. Cosier, whom a sports writer had once called as steady as a pebble, promptly juggled it, and what had looked like a double play fizzled into nothing. There were men on first and second now, and one out.

Mike got his fast one past the clean-up man. Then he got a good change-up in there, and the hitter chased it in vain. Now he had the big man in the hole and he teased around with two slow outside pitches that missed. The batter didn't stir.

Then he came in with the fast one. As he saw the ball rocket from the bat he knew it was gone. He turned and looked. It reached the top of the left-field wall and bounced over. Three runs came in.

The crowd was really on him now. Slick Hammill walked over to him and said, "Never mind that. The fans in this town are strictly bush."

Mike turned on him. "So are you," he said angrily. "Don't calm me down any more." He liked the fans in this town; they had always been his friends. He did not like Slick Hammill. Hammill went back to his position, looking outraged.

Mike then proceeded to get the side out. He got them out in the second, too, but first they loaded the bases on him, and only a leaping catch by Perutz saved him from another three-run attack. The Blues went out in order in both the first and the second.

In the top of the third Mike knew he'd had it. His fast ball was being hammered too much. Even when it wasn't banged back for a hit, it was banged. Some good fielding plays saved him temporarily, but with two men on and two men out, he threw a real gopher ball. It left the park, and now the Blues trailed, 0-6. Pops didn't take him out, because the bases were cleared now. He got the third out.

Mike was the third batter in the bottom of the third and as he waited for his turn he saw pitchers throwing, out in the Blues' bull pen. He got the idea he had pitched his last inning for that day.

The first Blue hitter was touched on the arm by a pitch and went to first—the first Blue runner of the game. The second one reached base on an error. Mike came to bat, and the entire attitude of the crowd suddenly changed.

"Come on, Mike!"

"You can do it, Mike!"

"All the way, Mike!"

It was almost as though he were two different people, as far as the crowd was concerned. They disliked the person on the mound and they liked the one at the plate. He couldn't fail to see how they felt.

The first pitch was a fast ball, tucked in under his chin. He didn't have to drop; he just slanted his body backward a little. But the familiar pattern was there. The pitcher didn't bother him. In the big leagues he would have been just another hurler, nothing special. He did have a sort of rough curve, which he shot by Mike on the second pitch. It didn't break until the last second, and Mike didn't realize it until too late. He also realized that the pitcher thought he had him overpowered with it.

In the big leagues, the pitcher would not have come right back with it. This man, though, was intent upon showing how he could handle a .348 hitter from the majors. He was used to fooling a batter twice in a row with the same pitch. He had never been in the big leagues, however, and Mike had.

Mike knew the same pitch was coming. He could read the young pitcher's mind. He took a slight step forward, swung, and caught the ball just before it took that nasty last-second break.

It was belted into the back yard of a machine-tool factory, far beyond the left-field fence. Everybody trotted. Everybody shook his hand. Pops Medlicott said to him, when he came in, "Beautiful, Mike. We're within reaching distance now. It's not your day out there on that mound. Give yourself a shower."

"I feel great," Mike said.

"I don't," Pops said. "The shower, Mike."

CHAPTER
27

MIKE looked up the newspaper that ran Ed Daly's column and saw that Daly had been fair to him—had quoted him accurately. Daly said a couple of things on his own which Mike wished he hadn't, but they didn't really rankle too much.

This is an amazing kid, this Mike Jaffe. On the surface you might say he is right in the stand he's always taken with the Sox, the fight he fought with the front office, and won. That is, he's trying to be true to himself, to be what he believes he is. Yet such a waste of natural talent has never met these old eyes in twenty-five years of covering those machinelike champs, the Blue Sox. The chances are, if Mike sticks to his guns down there where night ball is king and the steaks are a little tougher, we might get another look at him again in this town. We might, and then again we may have to comb the pages of *The Sporting News* in five years to learn whether he's holding his own with Valdosta or Schenectady. Meanwhile, the memory of Mike Jaffe taking a full cut at a baseball will linger long in the minds of Blue Sox fans, including this reporter.

Then Ed Daly added a final paragraph in which he quoted Stan Davis. The Sox general manager, in a later interview, had said:

"To my mind, Mike Jaffe was the best natural hitter to come through our system since Russ Woodward, and I can't say much more than that. However, as you may remember, when Woodward didn't fit into our type of baseball, we let him go. He came back, and you know what he's meant to this club ever since. We have farm clubs loaded with talent, although I don't see another Jaffe on the horizon at the moment. But if there is one thing that is expendable with the Blue Sox, it is talent. Our men must fit in with our preconceived notions of what makes a pennant-winning ball club. Jaffe didn't."

Mike read, farther down the page, that an out-fielder named Moses Malone had been recalled from another Sox farm club to spell Luke Bates. He remembered Moses Malone from several spring-training camps. He was a big man who could hit for distance but was slow afoot, hit into too many double plays, and often struck out.

Mike knew now that the Sox would never make a move to bring him back. He was sure that they would give him every chance to prove himself as a pitcher. But the trouble was that he began to realize how very much more confidence he had in himself as a hitter than as a pitcher.

Well, he had most of August and all of September to prove himself with the Blues.

By Labor Day Mike had won two and lost three, but he had failed to finish a single game. Pops Medlicott had never once asked him to play in the outfield and he had used Mike only twice as a pinch hitter. The fans didn't hoot at him any more and the players didn't rib him. He realized that he had become quite an unimportant figure.

He followed the Blue Sox every day in the papers. They had tailed off. After taking that double-header from the Clippers, they had lost the next two games of the series and had left town exactly as they had entered it, a game and a half ahead. Going into their Labor Day double-header, they were back in second place, one full game out. The Clippers were in first again, and the Redskins were crowding the Sox from behind.

Moses Malone was a bust, which didn't surprise Mike. He was batting .237 and was never used except when Luke Bates needed a rest. Luke was holding up well, though; he was still hitting in the .290's. Jug Slavin was back at his old practice of using a different clean-up hitter every third or fourth game. Woodward seemed to be headed toward the league record for receiving the greatest number of intentional bases on balls.

Mike found himself staying in the batting cage longer and longer, taking all the cuts he could. He had given up his slider entirely. It wasn't effective in the tight spots. He told Pops Medlicott what he was doing.

Pops nodded. "I never approved of it," he said. "There's plenty of time for that cute stuff once your fast one is gone. Yours isn't."

His fast one wasn't gone, but it wasn't exactly overpowering the batters. His curve was all right, though not spectacular, but actually his change-up was his best pitch. He used it often, almost like a crutch. The trouble was, however, that the opposing batters were beginning to realize this and know when to look for it.

The Blues were starting a three-game series—night games—with the Colts, and Mike was due to pitch the first one. While he was warming up he saw an unhappily familiar figure emerge from the tunnel and head toward him, on the way to the Colts' bench. It was Fritz Wesson.

Mike held his next warm-up toss and stared. His warm-up catcher, Joe Eula, walked over to him. "What's up?" Eula asked. "You feel all right?"

Mike nodded. "That guy, the one that just came out of the tunnel—he looks like a pitcher I used to know. Fritz Wesson."

"Don't you read the local papers?" Eula said. "The Colts just bought him from some Double-A club down South. Used to be with the Clippers."

"I know," Mike said.

"Oh!" Eula said. "Now I remember. He's the one you slugged, the one that—"

"He's the one," Mike said. "Come on, let's go."

[193]

He was tossing them in as Fritz Wesson walked by. The dark little pitcher with the mean twist to his mouth needed a shave, as always. He paused to watch Mike a moment. "Well, well!" he said. "Look who's here."

"Hello, Wesson," Mike said, holding the ball in his hand a moment.

"Don't bother saying hello to me and I won't bother saying hello to you. Except for you, I wouldn't be here."

Mike didn't reply. He was thinking that except for Wesson he probably wouldn't be here either.

"I notice you never picked any fights with the big pitchers," Wesson sneered.

Mike pitched again. Wesson still didn't move.

"I hear they had you spending all your time batting dirt off your pants," Wesson said.

Mike turned. "Beat it," he said, "or I'll hit you harder than I did the last time."

Wesson started to go. Over his shoulder he called back, "You're real tough, like a cream puff. The next time I get a chance to give you a shave I'll *really* shave you, Junior."

Mike wished he hadn't run into Wesson. He was still seeing his sneering face, hearing his sneering voice, when he threw the first ball to the first Colt batter. Wesson had been labeled a dirty pitcher all around the league; it was only his bean balls that had kept him in the majors the few years he had lasted there. Mike knew that if he hadn't finally hit Wesson, somebody else would have done it.

His first pitch was very wide. As he took the toss back from Eula, he heard Wesson's voice cut across the infield, from the Colts' dugout. "You're not even a good busher, Jaffe!"

Mike tried to stop listening, but Wesson's piercing voice couldn't be shut out. Jibe followed jibe. Mike walked two men. A sacrifice put them on second and third. He walked the fourth man intentionally. Then Cosier let a line drive that he should have had go past him, to his right. It went straight down the left-field line, a double that cleaned the bases. With Madigan covering third, Mike couldn't help thinking, it would have been a simple double play.

Wesson kept needling him. His remarks grew more insulting. Once Mike made a move toward the bench, but Cosier and Eula intercepted him. The umpire went over and warned Wesson. It didn't matter. Mike lasted only three innings, and he left two on, no one out, and the Blues behind, 0-5.

This was the seventh straight game he had failed

to finish. Of course, he had won a couple, and there had been times when he had felt he was in charge. Actually, though, he knew there were at least three other pitchers on the Blues' staff whom Pops would pick ahead of him for a key game.

The next night he stayed in the batting cage so long, whenever it was his turn, that Perutz had to ask him to get out of there. He went out and shagged flies every minute that he was not in the cage. And when the opposing pitchers started to warm up, and he saw Fritz Wesson was due to pitch for the Colts, he went over to Pops Medlicott. "Pops," he said, "I've got a favor to ask you."

"Sure, Mike."

"Can I play left field tonight?"

Pops peered at him over his rimless glasses, in that curious uncritical way of his. "What brought this up?" he asked.

"Can I, Pops?"

"But why, all of a sudden?"

"I want to bat again against that Wesson."

Pops barely touched his arm. "You're in left field, Mike. You're batting clean-up."

CHAPTER

28

THE BLUES went out in order against Fritz Wesson in the first, so Mike didn't get a chance to face him then. Out in left field the fans were surprisingly friendly. There was no jeering, nothing but encouragement. It was nice to hear them pulling for him again.

"How to go, Mike!"

"About time you got back where you belong, Mike!"

"Hit a couple tonight, Mike!"

The second Colt hitter in the second inning drove a long one to his left. It wasn't a tough catch, really, but it took some running and a final stab. But the crowd acted as though it had been a great catch. The left-field fans stood up and applauded Mike as he returned to his position. He felt a small but definite glow. He had the feeling that he had come back home, after a trip into the wilderness.

Mike batted first in the top of the second. He saw Fritz Wesson do a quick pantomime of a boxer sparring. The Colt catcher, whose unlikely name was Bill Brain, said to him, "You're the toughest-looking Little Leaguer I ever saw. A mass of brawn."

"You shut up," Mike said, "or you'll find out."

"Don't be frightened by Fritz," Brain said. "He won't hurt you—much."

Mike dug in. He planted his feet, brought the bat back, and went into his slight crouch. His wrists felt like iron. Wesson delivered. The ball was low and outside.

On the mound, Wesson laughed. Behind Mike, Brain snickered. "What're you jumping away from, sonny boy?" Brain asked.

Mike hadn't budged. He didn't reply.

Wesson threw one, right at his throat. Mike merely jumped back.

"Ho, ho!" Brain said derisively.

Mike didn't look at Brain, but he did turn his head slightly. "You tell Wesson for me, the next time he comes close to my head he's in trouble."

"Ah, now," Brain said, "you play too rough."

The pitch came in high, but not close. Mike let it go by. The next one came in belt-high and inside, and he whaled it. It went through the glow of the lights, over the technicolor green of the outfield, into the deep hole between left and center. Mike plowed around first, around second, and went into third with a slide that no one challenged.

He stood up, batting the dirt from his pants, and called to Wesson, "Still batting dirt from my pants, Wesson."

Wesson didn't deign to glance his way until he went into his stretch. Mike shot down the line as he did. Wesson had his foot on the rubber, but he turned, in panic, and threw to third base. The umpire called a balk, and Mike walked in.

There was a furious argument, led by Wesson and seconded by Brain and the Colt manager. It was to no avail. Everyone on the Blue bench was waiting for Mike as he came in, and they slapped him and pounded him on the back.

Wesson was wobbly after that, but he was still in there in the fourth. He was behind, 3-1, with men on second and third and one out. He walked Cosier, who batted ahead of Mike. The roar from the crowd made it clear they were very happy that Wesson was facing Mike again.

Mike knew what was coming; he was sure of it. The first pitch from Wesson backed up his certainty. It was a rifle shot, high and so close to the head that a pheasant would have had a hard time getting out of its way. Mike did, though, and he didn't drop; he fell back, shoved his bat behind him, and remained on his feet. Then he took three steps toward the mound, stopped, and called, "One more. Just one more, Wesson, and we'll give you what you're asking for."

Mike could see the enraged look on Wesson's face. He went back to the box and dug in again. He heard the umpire mumble something, but he couldn't make out what it was. Brain, from his crouch, snapped, "Here's where we separate the Boy Scouts from the lumberjacks."

"You're dead right," Mike said.

The next ball was low and outside. Mike thought of swinging at it, but he really wanted to give Wesson all the leeway he wanted. This thing between them had to be settled, once and for all. If Wesson failed to throw another pitch at his head, the victory would be Mike's. If Wesson did throw another at his head, Mike wouldn't have won yet, but he wouldn't have lost, either.

Wesson threw another one at his head. This time

Mike had to drop. He got up, slung his bat away, and strode toward the mound. Brain had thrown the ball back to Wesson, and Wesson had it in his hand. Mike kept advancing. He was aware that players from both benches were rushing toward him, but he did not stop. He was within a few feet of Wesson, when suddenly Wesson threw the ball at him. It hit him on the shoulder and glanced off. He advanced no farther.

Wesson turned and fled. He disappeared inside the Colt dugout, so fast that he might have been a sparrow. The crowd was roaring, laughing, jeering —at Wesson.

It was a good night for Mike, all in all. In addition to the triple, he came up with a single and two walks, and one line drive that turned into an out when the Colt shortstop looked, for the moment, like Andy Pearson. After the game nobody said much to him, but they all gave him some quick slaps on the back as they went by his locker.

In the steaming shower room, Perutz said, "It's a good thing Wesson ran. I had a feeling you'd break him in two."

"I think I would have," Mike said. "With no regrets."

"He's a miserable character, anyway," Perutz said.

Mike shrugged. "Pitchers are more miserable than most people. I know. I was one once. Why is it?"

"Search me," Perutz said.

THE next morning Mike, as usual, bought the paper that told what the Blue Sox had done the day before. This, in part, was what he read:

Yesterday a true baseball hero died. In the ninth inning the Blue Sox had a one-run lead. The Panthers put men on first and third with two outs. The Sox were in a dead heat with the Clippers for first place. The Clippers had already won their ball game; the scoreboard showed that. If the Sox lost this one, they would be back in second. If they won it, they would stay tied.

This fact was no doubt in the mind of every man on the Blue Sox team. The Blue Sox pitcher, crafty Eddie Lasky, threw one that a Panther pinch hitter named Harold Beane found to his liking. He drilled it, and it went out somewhere in the wide open spaces that stretch between left and center. It looked for all the world as if the Sox were back in second place.

They were not, however. From the deep recesses of nowhere came, not the young and agile Woodward, but the old and bent Luke Bates. To describe what Bates did is impossible. Suffice it to say that he climbed the wall and somehow, someway, got one glove partly in front of that plainly labeled triple. He conked his head, he conked his shoulders; in fact, he conked out. But when they picked him up the ball was frozen inside his glove. It was there, and the ball game was over. Bates was taken off the field on a stretcher. The Sox were still tied for first place with the Clippers.

Examination at the hospital showed a lot of things about the thirty-nine-year-old Bates that indicated he was through for the season. It may even be that Bates is through, period—and exclamation point. There went one of the hardest-fighting ballplayers of this era, and he went gloriously, with his glove on.

Now, of course, the Sox are still tied for first place, and they have a dilemma: they don't have

Bates. They have Moses Malone and Bob Blossom, and they have nearly a month to go. They are tied for first place. But Malone and Blossom don't add up to Bates.

When Mike finished reading this, he went to find Pops Medlicott. He cornered Pops and said, "Do you think the Sox would take me back? I read about Luke Bates."

"Take you back as what?" Pop said. "Pitcher? Bat boy? Clubhouse man?"

"Left fielder," Mike said.

"I'm glad you brought the matter up," Pops said. "Now that you mention it, it occurs to me there just might be a chance for you. A slight chance. But a chance."

"Will you phone and ask?" Mike said.

"You sit right where you are," Pops said.

After an interminable time Pops came back. "I talked with Jug Slavin," he said.

"Did you tell him I asked to come back?"

"I did that," Pops said.

"What did he say, Pops?"

"He wanted to know about your pitching first. I told him it was terrible and that I thought you knew it was."

Mike nodded eagerly.

"I told him you got plunked by Wesson yesterday and that you almost hauled off and broke him apart."

Mike nodded again.

"Jug said, 'If he feels that way, put him on the first plane you can get him on.'"

Mike blinked. "When does it go?"

Pops stood up. "Let's go find out."

CHAPTER
30

MIKE didn't learn, until he reached the Blue Sox clubhouse early the next afternoon, that it was Old Timers' Day at the Stadium. He found the place deserted, even though it was a couple of hours before game time. Only Pickles was there.

Pickles looked at him. "You again?" Pickles said.

"Me again," Mike said.

"You know the locker," Pickles said. "I'll get you a uniform."

"Where is everybody?" Mike asked.

Pickles turned on him as though he had asked an immoral question. "Where would they be? Watching the great ones, of course. Don't you know it's Old Timers' Day?"

"What's that?" Mike asked.

Pickles put his hands on his hips. "Listen. Out on that field, right now, are the greatest Blue Soxers that ever pulled on a uniform. You should be happy to belong here. I'll get your uniform. Then I'm going up to watch."

When Pickles got the uniform, he almost flung it at Mike. Mike put it down on the bench in front of his locker and watched Pickles move out. He got dressed, hearing the subdued roar of what could only be a packed house up above. Then he went through the tunnel, following the string of unshaded bulbs, until he reached the rim of the playing field. He stood there, leaning against the wall, in the shelter of the tunnel. Out on the field he saw the greatest of the Blue Sox, from way back. Some of them he recognized from pictures.

On first was Marty (Beef Trust) Blake. On second was Tommy Shore, and at shortstop was Patsy Bates. Mike didn't recognize the man on third, because he was before Madigan's time, and Madigan went as far back as he could remember, even with the help of pictures.

In right field was the greatest Blue Sox slugger of them all—Augie Marshall. Mike remembered, as a kid, reading about the rough time Chip Fiske had had, when he'd been pulled up from the farm system to replace this giant of a slugger, who had been traded. It turned out that Marshall was over the hill, and Chip had finally made his own place.

In center field was another legendary Blue Sox player, Vic Valenti. For many, many years Vic had patrolled that sector, before Russ Woodward had come along, and Vic had been just about everything a center fielder should be. Fast as lightning and always getting the jump on the ball. In his time Vic had batted third in the Sox order.

In left field was the incomparable Kennie Willard. Willard had made history, and not just baseball history. He had been the first Negro to break down the outdated racial barriers in what had been called the great American game. After Kennie, the game had really become American.

There was old Tweet Tillman, the most durable catcher in the league, squatting behind the plate. He still was going strong as a coach. The pitcher was a player Mike didn't know.

It was only a two-inning game, and the score was now 1-1. The modern Sox were batting, with two out. Russ Woodward lofted one deep to center. Valenti, no doubt creaking in every bone, went back and back and demonstrated to a certain extent why he had been on nine All-Star teams. He flipped his glove in a backhand stab, and pulled the ball in.

Now it was the home team's half of the second and last inning. The first batter was the fabulous Augie Marshall. This, Mike wanted to see; he had heard and read so much about him. He was thicker through the middle now, but you could see that he'd been a terror, just by the way he swung, and missed, the first pitch. The second pitch came in there, for nobody was trying to strike anybody out—certainly not Harry Diefendorf, who was carrying the honors at the moment. Augie gave it the full treatment.

His swing was something beautiful to watch. He met the ball, because it really had nothing much on it, and it rose. It went out so far that an eagle would have given up the chase. Finally it settled in the seats, maybe a dozen rows back. The crowd was happy. So was Mike. He had heard so much about Augie Marshall, and now he knew what everyone had been talking about.

He went down to the dressing room again, feeling a little bit proud and a little bit humble that he had been chosen to belong to this club. He sat on the bench in front of his locker for quite a while before he heard the old familiar clatter of spikes on the floor. He looked up.

"Hey!" Madigan yelled. "Look who's here!"

"The kid!" Fiske said.

"Where you been, boy?" Gibbs asked, patting him on the shoulder as he went by.

"I'm back, that's all," Mike said.

"This one," Lasky said, "keeps going up and down like a Yo-yo."

Mike saw Jug come into the room, with Stan Davis right behind him. Jug looked around, spied Mike, and jerked his thumb toward his office. Mike nodded, got up, and followed. When he entered, Jug and Stan Davis stared at him in a way that made him feel he was some sort of buried treasure, just pried off the ocean's bottom.

"Now look, Mike," Jug said, as the three of them sat down. "The time for fooling is past. You're here to stay, or if you're not you'll never come back again. Which do you want it to be?"

"I'm here to stay," Mike said.

"You're an outfielder?"

"I'm an outfielder," Mike said.

"How do you know that? You never did before."

"Because I *want* to be an outfielder."

"What made you want to be one?"

Mike thought a moment. "I decided I was a lousy pitcher, for one thing," he said.

"That's enough," Jug said. "Hold the rest."

"Can I get in the line-up today?" Mike asked.

"You're in," Jug said.

Stan Davis, who had started prowling around the room as usual, broke in. "You know who's pitching for the Clippers today?"

"No."

"Wilcy Lord. You remember Wilcy Lord?"

"Like I remember a case of measles," Mike said. "He won't knock me down twice again."

"Son, you sound different."

"All I want to know is, can I play?"

Jug said, "You already asked that and I already answered it. You're in."

"Baby," Stan Davis said, "welcome back."

The G.M. held out his hand. Mike shook it and turned to go. "I just remembered something," he said.

He left the office, went to his locker, and dug out his two gloves. He saw Artie, the bat boy, across the room and called to him. Artie came over. "You want a glove?" Mike asked.

"Sure," Artie said.

Mike picked up his pitcher's glove with the stubby fingers and tossed it to Artie. "All yours," he said. "It's an old one and I'm through with it."

CHAPTER

31

MIKE heard the happy yell the capacity crowd let out when his name came over the loud-speaker system as the left fielder, batting clean-up. When he trotted out to take his position, the fans shouted to him from the nearby stands.

"Mike's back!"

"Murder 'em, Mike!"

"Come on, Mike, boy!"

Joe Rodriguez was going for the Sox today. Crafty Joe had a way of threading his pitches, rather than pouring them in. When he was right, he had batters either hitting his curve ball on the ground or popping it up, though he never overpowered them. Today he was right, if the first inning told the story.

Three Clippers in a row grounded out or popped up. Inside the dugout, the Sox were full of chatter, all cheerful and confident. Before he ducked inside, Mike saw the Blue Sox old-timers sitting right behind the dugout. He knew he was probably being watched by them with special interest, because they had never seen him before. And probably whatever reports they had read had not been too good.

Madigan sliced a sinking line drive to right field and it fell in for a well-earned single. Fiske bunted him to second. Woodward topped a roller down the third-base line and, with his fine speed, beat it out. Mike stepped in and there was a friendly buzz, not exactly a roar, from the stands.

"The commuter," Berry said, in a barely audible snicker.

"I gave it up," Mike said. "Decided to settle down a while. Here."

"Watch out for Wilcy," Berry said. "You know how rough he is on growing boys."

Wilcy Lord checked his runners and went into the stretch. The ball came in hard and high. It didn't knock Mike down, but it brushed him back from the plate. He heard the buzz in the stands turn into an angry-sounding swell of noise. Wilcy grinned. He threw a second one just as high, just as hard, and even closer. Mike fell back from it, but he didn't go down.

"Same old patsy," Berry said.

Mike waited. He saw the ball coming in. It was belt-high, on the extreme outside corner. He slid his hands down the bat, faced it toward first, and trickled a bunt beautifully up the first-base line.

Lord was over, quick as a fox, but the ball was right on the base path. Mike didn't slow down the churning of his legs for a moment. Wilcy was fielding the bunt right in his path, just as he had planned —and just as everyone in the park knew, by now, that he had planned. Mike crashed into Lord full force. The little southpaw went careening over backward like a barrel hit by a bulldozer. The ball squirted out of his hands and rolled back toward the pitcher's mound. Frantically the Clipper second baseman and shortstop raced after it, leaving second base uncovered.

Madigan had strolled in from third and Woodward was on his way there like a greyhound. Mike went into second base unmolested. And the club trainer was out looking Wilcy Lord over, as he sat up on the infield grass and blinked his eyes in astonishment. When the consultation ended, Lord was led to the dugout by the trainer and

[215]

Shanty Milligan. Somebody was hurriedly warming up in the Clipper bull pen. It turned out to be Ron Marsen, who had been scheduled to pitch later in the series.

It was clear that Marsen hadn't had a chance to get fully warmed up. He walked Pete Gibbs intentionally and then walked Andy Pearson unintentionally, to force in the second run. Stretch Stookey tied into the first pitch and slammed it to the base of the wall in right center for a triple that cleaned the bases. The Sox were out in front, 5-0.

The game was a rout right there in the first inning. Shanty Milligan hastily pulled Marsen out and called for Bub Gram, his best reliever, whom he usually saved for late-inning spots.

But there was no stopping the Sox now. No Clipper pitchers seemed to be ready, and all the Sox hitters were. Walker singled Stookey in, and then Rodriguez struck out, but Madigan and Fiske kept things going with two more walks. Woodward dribbled a single through the hole at short and another run came in. The bases were filled as Mike came up for the second time in the inning.

No pitch of Gram's came even close to his head. Mike stood there and took three straight balls, all low and outside. Then he got the hit sign from Tweet

Tillman on the three-and-nothing pitch, and he hit away.

To Mike's ears, the ball seemed to sing as it went off the fat part of his bat in one of those rising line drives headed deep toward left. It just missed clearing the wall, hit the top, and bounced back in. He was on second with a stand-up double, the bases were cleared, and the Sox were now in front 10-0 in the first inning.

When Mike went in to get his glove, Jug Slavin was waiting to hand it to him. "You better buy yourself a second glove one of these days," Jug said. "All the regulars keep two, just in case."

"I had two," Mike said, "but I gave one away. It was the wrong kind. I'll get another spare—the right kind."

"Looks like we're back in first place," Jug said.

"And this time to stay," Mike said.

He headed out toward left field at a dogtrot and saw that the crowd in the left-field stands were already on their feet, waiting to greet him. It occurred to him, as he passed the infield skin, that the distance to the left-field wall wasn't very far. He had the idea that he would bang a lot of baseballs off that wall before he came back some day to play in an Old Timers' game.

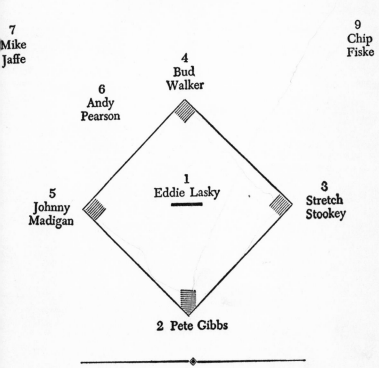

8
Russ Woodward

7
Mike
Jaffe

9
Chip
Fiske

4
Bud
Walker

6
Andy
Pearson

1
Eddie Lasky

3
Stretch
Stookey

5
Johnny
Madigan

2 Pete Gibbs

1 STARTING PITCHER

2 THE CATCHER FROM DOUBLE-A

3 THE BIG STRETCH

4 FAST MAN ON A PIVOT

5 GOOD FIELD, NO HIT

6 MISTER SHORTSTOP

7 LONG BALL TO LEFT FIELD

8 SWITCH HITTER

9 HIT AND RUN

onsin State College at Eau Claire
LIBRARY RULES

No   k should be taken from the library until
it ha   en properly charged by the librarian.
            may be kept one week but are not to
            ed without special permission of the

            of two cents a day will be charged for
            pt over time.
            e of loss or injury the person borrowing
            will be held responsible for a part or the
            the value of a new book.

	DUE	DUE	DUE
Feb	JUN 26 '68		
1	OCT 14 '68		
APR 13	Nov 13		
MAR 30			
APR 2	MAR 4 '69		
JUL	MAY 13 '69		
DEC 7	Jul 7		
NOV 13	JUN 27 '71		
JUN 2	OCT 21 '71		
NOV			
JUN			
JUN			
FEB			
APR			